They were celebrating a wedding anniversary

It was common knowledge that Kostas hadn't expected his friend's marriage to a foreigner to thrive.

"The father," Kostas whispered, "has just finished telling the happy couple that a good marriage is like good wine—sweet to the taste, heady to the senses and better with time." He eyed Nancy thoughtfully. "How is it that you have remained single?"

"In America we wait for the right person to come along," Nancy replied self-consciously. Although she had wanted Kostas to display an interest in her, now she found herself wanting him to change the subject.

"Sometimes it is difficult to know who is the right one." His face hardened. "That is why an arranged match often succeeds where romantic marriages fail—despite my friend's good luck."

Was he issuing a warning, Nancy wondered.

WELCOME
TO THE WONDERFUL WORLD
OF *Harlequin Romances*

Interesting, informative and entertaining,
each Harlequin Romance portrays an appealing
and original love story. With a varied array
of settings, we may lure you on an African safari,
to a quaint Welsh village, or an exotic Riviera
location—anywhere and everywhere that adventurous
men and women fall in love.

As publishers of Harlequin Romances, we're
extremely proud of our books. Since 1949,
Harlequin Enterprises has built its publishing
reputation on the solid base of quality and
originality. Our stories are the most popular
paperback romances sold in North America; every
month, six new titles are released and sold at
nearly every book-selling store in Canada and the
United States.

For a list of all titles currently available,
send your name and address to:

HARLEQUIN READER SERVICE,
(In the U.S.) 901 Fuhrmann Blvd.
P.O. Box 1325, Buffalo, NY 14269
(In Canada) P.O. Box 2800, Postal Station A,
5170 Yonge St., Willowdale, Ont. M2N 6J3

We sincerely hope you enjoy reading
this Harlequin Romance.

Yours truly,

THE PUBLISHERS
Harlequin Romances

Aegean Enchantment

Emily Francis

Harlequin Books

TORONTO • NEW YORK • LONDON
AMSTERDAM • PARIS • SYDNEY • HAMBURG
STOCKHOLM • ATHENS • TOKYO • MILAN

ISBN 0-373-02757-5

Harlequin Romance first edition April 1986

CHAPTER ONE

IT WAS THE THIRD GRAY wet day in a row. Yet it was April, and spring should have come by this time, Nancy Spaulding thought glumly. She peered out of the train window and felt her normally cheerful spirits flagging with each mile; month after dreary month of bitter cold and snow had been followed not by crocuses and forsythia, but by rain and muddy slush.

"April is the cruelest month," she thought, as the line from a poem she had studied in school came back to her. It was particularly cruel this year, she decided, because it was just another wintry month and failed to herald the warm weather she longed for.

The train sped past the crowded tenements marking the outskirts of the city. Lately the trip to New York from her sister Jan's home in Connecticut seemed longer, and the crowded city more depressing. Perhaps it was because of the strain she had been under.

As the train roared into Grand Central Station, Nancy automatically stood and put on her trench coat. Out of force of habit she joined the stream of Brooks Brothers-suited young executives and hurriedly stepped onto the platform heading for the Forty-second Street exit. A casual observer would not have guessed her state of mind, for her trim athletic five-foot-four figure moved with agility and vigor, and her head, with its mass of fawn-colored curls, was held high. Only those who knew her well might have noticed the hint of sadness in her usually lively hazel eyes.

She pulled her collar up around her neck and opened her umbrella against the rain outside the station. Squaring her shoulders, she strode briskly toward the bus that would take her on the final stage of the daily journey to her job as physical therapist at the Truman Medical Center.

Propelled along the slick sidewalks by the crowds of work-bound people, Nancy quickly reached the bus stop. Impatient bodies crowded around her. Catching their mood, Nancy glanced at her watch. The bus was late. She sighed, unable to dispel the depression that had taken hold of her when she had realized there would be no escape from the dreary city for months or even years.

Two months ago she had gone home to find her sister sitting forlornly with red-rimmed eyes in the kitchen. Nancy's heart had quickened with dread when she saw the despair written on Jan's face.

"Jan, what is it?" she cried.

And her sister—the older sister who had been more like a mother to her, who had sent her through school—collapsed in tears on her shoulder. Between sobs, Jan told her that her husband, Burt, had been laid off work. Nancy knew what that meant. With Burt's income gone, Jan would have to pay all the bills, instead of her usual share. In the weeks that followed, Nancy had had to count pennies. There were no more evenings out with her friends, no more dinners and movies with her colleagues. And to make matters worse, Jan suffered from bronchitis, which meant that Nancy was responsible for the children and the house more often than not. The result was exhaustion.

Nancy felt no resentment about her situation, believing as she did that in times of trouble families should stick together. Yet she did wish she could be more like her friends, who were already making plans for their summer vacations. There would be no vacation for her.

The bus screeched to a stop at the curb, and Nancy shook herself back to reality. The bus was overheated and jammed with commuters fighting for seats. Nancy was forced to stand, hanging on to a strap with her free hand and swaying with the lurching movements of the bus as it lumbered its way through the Manhattan traffic. With an effort, she pushed her problems out of her mind and concentrated on her favorite young patient, Niko Paradissis.

The Greek boy was the one bright spot in her life. As she thought about him, her mouth curved into a smile and she forgot about the woman behind her who was jabbing her with her purse. Niko was sweet and good-natured in spite of a serious spinal injury that caused him considerable pain. He had spent months in an Athens hospital before being brought to New York to be treated by the world-famous Dr. Randall Davies. The surgery had been successful, and now it was her jób to retrain the boy in the use of his limbs and to restore his wasted muscles.

Over the months he had become more than just a patient to her. Seeing this, Dr. Davies had gradually cut down her other duties so she could spend more of her time with Niko. Like the best of doctors, Davies was keenly aware of the psychological component in a successful cure.

Her stop came, and she pushed her way out through the unyielding bodies that blocked the door, still caught up in thoughts of Niko. He had been more than usually cheerful this week because of news he had received from home. After long weeks of isolation thousands of miles from his family and friends, with only his widowed father as company, he was at last expecting a visitor from Greece.

He had received Kostas's letter exactly one week ago, Nancy remembered, and the change in his attitude was immediate. He began exercising too enthusiastically. She tried to explain to him that while his muscles were strengthening from long disuse, the connective tissues had to be coaxed gently into regaining their resiliency or serious damage could result. But his boyish excitement was catching, and soon she stopped chiding him and let him give in to his high spirits, listening to him happily chattering away. It seemed every other word was "Kostas," and his thoughts revolved around the reunion with his wonderful brother.

Kostas was older than Niko by eighteen years, and to hear Niko tell it he was the best older brother any boy could have. Some boys made heroes of cowboys or baseball players or racing drivers, but Kostas put these figures to shame in Niko's eyes. Nancy took his extravagant praise with a grain of salt. According to the boy, his brother was the best driver, the best soccer player, the best swimmer and the best diver in the whole world.

And today, Nancy thought as she climbed the rain-slick steps and entered the vast echoing hall of the hospital, Kostas would be arriving. She envied the boy his excitement, wishing she could be as enthusiastic about something as Niko was about this visit. She was sure he had had a sleepless night in anticipation, while she had had an equally sleepless night taking care of her sister's sick child. Even meeting the Olympian Kostas Paradissis couldn't relieve her of her oppressive responsibilities.

She took the elevator up to the third floor and hung her wet coat on a hook in the staff lounge. Then she went along the hall to Niko's room.

She found the eleven-year-old in bed looking pale. His usually animated body was listless, and his face had a sunken look she had not seen before. He was holding a letter in his hands, a letter he apparently had reread several times.

"It is from Kostas," he said without giving her his customarily enthusiastic greeting.

Nancy felt her own spirits sink even lower at his tone and she knew what was in the letter. She felt his disappointment keenly.

"He tells me he is very busy. He has much business to do because papa is here in New York with me. He will have to travel to Germany this week. He will not come to see me."

This time it was impossible to ignore the unhappy note, almost like a sob, in his voice. The sweet olive-skinned face trembled, and tears gathered behind his eyelids.

Going quickly to his bedside, she sat next to him and took his hand. "He'll come another time, Niko. I'm certain he'll come."

"Yes," the child said quickly, trying to hide his hurt face from her. "He will be sure to come soon."

Nancy reached out and took his chin in her hand. "Why are you turning away from me, Niko? Don't you think I'm a good-enough friend to understand that you feel hurt? You can trust me, you know."

"I know," he said softly, the tears slowly beginning to make their way down his cheeks. "There is no reason to hide my sorrow from you, Nancy." He turned his trusting face up to her, his large dark eyes brimming over. "But Kostas would say I am not behaving like a man."

"Kostas is quite wrong," she answered severely, handing him a tissue. "When people are hurt, tears come all by themselves. Doesn't your brother know that men are allowed to cry, too?"

Her words seemed to allow him to release his tears. When he was done crying, he wiped his eyes and blew his nose.

"But of course Kostas *is* very busy," he said. "Kostas has taken over most of papa's business, and so he has much to do."

Nancy's lips were set in a hard line as she pulled back the covers on the bed and helped Niko up. She saw through his excuses and felt that an import business, no matter how large or important, was not a real excuse. What kind of a man was this Kostas, anyway? How could he fail the brother who adored him? Was this what expectation and trust and hope had come to? If Kostas Paradissis had any idea of how much his visit meant to Niko, he must be hardhearted indeed, she thought. She ached for the boy, knowing something of disappointment herself. Yet the excuse he made for his brother made him dearer to her than ever, and she felt eager to reward him in some way, to make up for his brother's obvious indifference.

"Tell you what, Niko," she said. "Why don't we postpone our exercises for a little and play checkers? You've been beating me lately, and I want to catch up."

"But look, Nancy," Niko said, not quite ready to leave the subject of his brother, "here is a photograph Kostas has sent me. Here he is on one of our boats. See how beautiful our sea is? It is the color of turquoise, is it not?"

Nancy took the picture from him and studied the tall well-built man in it. Kostas was decidedly attractive, with the same thick dark hair and large fluid eyes that Niko had. But unlike his young brother, he had an unmistakable expression of arrogance, especially around the mouth and in the haughty way he held his head. She felt an instinctive dislike for the man. He looked like just the sort of man, she thought angrily, who would put his own convenience above the happiness of an eleven-year-old child.

Saying nothing of her true feelings, she handed the photo back to Niko, who propped it lovingly up on the bedside table.

"Enough stalling, my friend," Nancy told him with mock severity. "Get out the checkerboard."

By early afternoon, as Niko finished his leg exercises, he was once more almost cheerful. He was chattering about *his* island when the head nurse stuck her gray head in through the doorway.

"Miss Spaulding, Dr. Davies would like to see you in his office."

Smoothing her white uniform, Nancy went down the hall, anxiously wondering what could have prompted the unusual summons. She tapped on the door of Dr. Randall Davies's office, and at his pleasant "Come in," she entered.

"Nancy, please sit down," he said. "I'll be with you in a moment."

After making some final notes to a patient's chart, he shut the folder and sat back in his leather chair, his large hands clasped in front of him on the desk.

"And how are you?" he asked, peering at her from behind his glasses.

When a member of the medical profession asked that question, it was not to be polite, she knew.

"I'm fine," she replied uneasily, anxious to find out what was on his mind.

"Hmm, yes." He studied her face. "A trifle pale. And I believe you've lost some weight. You work much too hard, young lady." He waved his pipe for emphasis. "A girl your age could do with a few months of new sights and a little sun. Put some roses into those pretty cheeks."

She was surprised at the unexpected personal turn the conversation had taken.

"Is something wrong, Dr. Davies?" she asked apprehensively.

Amusement caused his homely face to crinkle into a network of fine lines. "No, my dear, on the contrary. I wanted to congratulate you on the fine work you've done with the Paradissis boy."

Nancy felt her tension dissolve and she returned his smile.

"In fact, Niko has come along so much better than we had first hoped, that I believe he'll be ready to return to Greece in a couple of weeks."

"A couple of weeks," Nancy repeated, knowing how Niko's disappointment would fade at such good news. "That'll make him so happy!"

And she was happy for him, thinking of all that he had suffered since his accident. But along with her pleasure she felt a sharp ache and realized how much she would miss him. It would be truly like losing a brother, for she had come to love the boy deeply.

"That doesn't mean, of course, that he's completely recovered, as you well know," the doctor continued, his face sobering. "He will require at least a month or two of therapy once he's home."

Nancy nodded. "Yes, of course."

The doctor leaned forward and tapped his pipe against the edge of the ashtray. "I had a talk with Niko's father this morning. Antonis Paradissis would like you to return to Greece with Niko and remain there for a while as his therapist. I wanted you to know that, should you accept, your job will be waiting for you when you return."

Greece! Nancy's heart quickened and she felt color flood into her cheeks. The photo of the Aegean and all the alluring descriptions of the island that Niko had poured out to her time and again in his homesickness sprung into her mind. To go to Greece would be a dream come true.

"It's funny," she said with a rueful little smile. "For twenty-three years nothing out of the ordinary has happened to me, and now I have an opportunity of a lifetime. I wish I could accept, but . . ." Her voice faltered.

"Yes?"

Nancy sighed, unaccustomed to discussing personal matters with the doctor.

"I'm afraid I couldn't leave home now, Dr. Davies. I live with my sister, you know. My brother-in-law lost his job recently, and they need me. I owe them so much."

"Pity," Dr. Davies said. "You've been so good with the boy. And as an employee of Antonis Paradissis, you undoubtedly would see Greece the way no tourist ever sees it. I spent a holiday there myself, many years ago, and I've always wanted to return. No people are more hospitable than the Greeks, I found."

Nancy stood, tears of frustration gathering in her eyes.

"I guess it's just not my fate," she said, hoping the doctor would not hear the quiver in her voice. "But I thank you, Dr. Davies, and please thank Mr. Paradissis for me."

It was time for her coffee break, but instead of sitting in the lounge with her friends, Nancy put on her coat and slipped outside, wanting to be alone. The rain had stopped, but the skies were still dark and the air was raw and oppressive. Everything looked gray and dismal, and the closed impersonal faces of the people she passed lowered her spirits even further.

Nancy crossed the street and reached the opposite curb only to have a jet of dirty water sprayed at her legs by a speeding taxi. At the river's edge she stood, hands in her pockets, watching barges plow through the murky water and, as though to torture herself, she thought again of the photograph Niko had shown her. The Aegean had looked, as Niko had often said, the color of turquoise, and behind the boat and its skipper towered craggy cliffs. Every fiber of her energetic, athletic young body longed to be climbing the rugged hills instead of standing here beneath skyscrapers, her feet in filthy rainwater. With a sigh, Nancy turned back.

I'm being childish, she told herself. *I have no reason to feel sorry for myself. I'm young and healthy and I have a good job I enjoy. If I can't go, I can't go.*

She knew she had to let go of her dreams and face reality. She owed it to Jan to see the family through its crisis.

At five-thirty, she bade Niko a fond good-night. The days were longer now, and dusk was just beginning to fall as she left the hospital. The afternoon with Niko had eased her depression somewhat, but coming out into the rain again, the thought of the long ride back to Stamford caused her heart to sink.

As she opened her umbrella, she felt a gentle hand on her arm.

"Miss Spaulding?"

She turned to face a uniformed chauffeur. "Yes?"

"Please." He gestured toward the gleaming Cadillac limousine parked at the curb. "Mr. Antonis Paradissis wishes to speak with you. Would you be so kind as to come with me?"

The back door of the car opened, and Nancy, hesitating only a moment, slid inside. The chauffeur closed the door after her, and a rich scent of tobacco and new leather enveloped her.

She had only met Niko's father a few times, and so her impression of the elderly importer was of a superficial nature. Although short in stature, as most Greeks were, he had an air of authority about him that spoke more plainly than words. Yet, on the one or two occasions they had exchanged words, he had been nothing but courteous. Now his hand grasped hers in a businesslike handshake.

"Miss Spaulding, I believe you are on your way to catch your train, yes?"

"Do you know my schedule, Mr. Paradissis?"

The swarthy lined face lifted in a smile. "I make it my business to know all about those with whom I work or with whom my sons are involved, and you are no exception. Now, with your permission, we shall talk while my chauffeur drives you to your home in Connecticut."

Looking into the heavily lidded charcoal eyes, Nancy knew her protests would be useless, and anyway, the luxury of the automobile was a welcome relief from the crowded bus and train. As the car pulled away from the curb, she leaned back into the soft leather of the seat and waited for whatever would come.

"You had a talk with Dr. Davies," Antonis Paradissis said, "and I believe that he told you of my offer."

"Yes, and I do thank you—" Nancy began, but he cut her off.

"Please, I do not wish your thanks. I wish to persuade you to change your mind."

The chauffeur was skillfully maneuvering the limousine through the congested city streets.

"Let me begin," Niko's father said, "by telling you that I am aware of what a great part you have played in my son's progress. And not only through Dr. Davies's reports. Niko is filled with praise. He considers you a very special friend, you know, and that is most important to me."

"I'm glad," Nancy replied, "because I feel the same about him. I'll miss him when he leaves," she added sincerely.

As though he had not heard her, the elderly man stared out of the window.

"Manhattan is a sad place for human beings to live. I always have this feeling when I come to New York. People do not belong so close to one another, with so much noise and so many automobiles. Now even Athens is beginning to resemble New York, and so I try to avoid Athens, too. I suppose I am an islander at heart, as are both my sons. We love nature. It is in the blood."

Nancy looked out and tried to see the city through his eyes. Concrete, crowded, inhuman. So different from the rocky hills and sparkling sea in the photograph.

"Niko is sweet and shy," Antonis Paradissis said, turning his attention away from the window, "like his mother."

A sigh escaped him, and Nancy knew that he must miss his dead wife.

"When such people form attachments, they are very dear. Niko is lonely, I am afraid. There had not been much pleasure for him since his accident, and so it has pleased me greatly to know that here in New York he has made such a good friend. He tells me you are even learning some Greek from him."

"Just about enough to order a glass of water in a restaurant," she laughed. "But Niko is very persistent about teaching me."

The older man smiled with pride. "Persistence. A family trait! Both Kostas and Niko are determined individuals. Even stubborn, one might say."

At the mention of Kostas, Nancy felt a surge of irritation. Selfish would be more accurate, she thought, but said nothing.

As the car sped along the turnpike to Connecticut, the man's dark eyes scrutinized Nancy in the light of passing cars.

"Miss Spaulding, I consider your presence as Niko's therapist essential to his recovery," he said in his former businesslike tone, "and I wish you to accompany Niko to our home in Korpas."

"Mr. Paradissis," Nancy answered, trying not to feel intimidated by him, "I'm very flattered and really grateful, but there is no way I can accept. I have family obligations—"

"Yes." He moved his gloved hand impatiently, as though brushing away a pesky fly.

"And anyway," Nancy cut in quickly before he could interrupt, "I'm sure there are many fine therapists in Greece who could work with Niko."

"But he wants you," the old man said simply, "and in my eyes that is the crucial factor. Now, Miss Spaulding, I have to leave for Athens in the morning and so I wish to conclude all our arrangements this evening."

"But, I—"

Antonis Paradissis stopped her with a look his business acquaintances would have known all too well—the look that always preceded a financial coup.

By the time the Cadillac turned off at the Stamford exit, the dismal picture Nancy Spaulding had had of her next few months was gone, for Antonis Paradissis had made so generous an offer that she could not refuse. Niko would benefit by her companionship, that was clear; and the financial arrangement he suggested would mean more money for Nancy's sister and her family than she could afford to give otherwise. Why, she practically had her ticket to Greece in her hands!

Dazed, Nancy stood in front of Jan's modest frame house, watching the car pull away. She stood rooted to the pavement as the realization sank in that she, who had never been farther away than New Jersey, would be leaving for Greece in two weeks. And then, after the car had turned the corner and disappeared from sight, she gave a spontaneous whoop of joy and raced up the front steps, two at a time, to tell the good news to Jan.

Who says dreams don't come true, sensible Nancy Spaulding asked herself.

CHAPTER TWO

SHE LEANED OVER the railing and watched the gentle Aegean curl up against the sides of the ferry. The Atlantic had never looked like this, so extraordinarily blue, not a whitecap in sight. Even though the port at Piraeus was well out of sight, and there was nothing to look at but sea and sky, Nancy felt she would never tire of the view before her now, or the feel of the wind whipping her hair, or the clear light that fell from a cloudless azure sky.

"You know, Niko, this is my first boat ride. I've never even been on the Staten Island ferry." She returned to her patient who sat on a cushioned bench against the cabin wall, out of the wind. "How wonderful it is. I could stay on board forever."

"Yes, you are a true sailor," Niko laughed. "That is, when the water is like glass. Try it again in February or March. Then even you would need your seasick pills."

"Oh, Niko, you *know* physical therapists are never sick!" She pulled his stocking cap down over his eyes. "Tell me, how long will it be before we see Korpas? I want to be sure to be out here, to see it as soon as it's visible."

Niko pushed his cap off one eye and peered at her. "The ship's agent said we would be at Korpas at four o'clock. That means we will be there at five." He pushed the cap back to its proper position.

"How do you know that?"

"It is an art, telling the time in my country. You must first guess about the captain's mood to see if the boat will go slow or fast today. Also, there are two small islands before Korpas, and there is much cargo to load. We will be delayed."

"And how do you know there is a lot of cargo?" She had done nothing but ask questions of him ever since she knew she was coming to Greece. There was so much she wanted to know, and fortunately, Niko was happy in his role of teacher.

"It is cucumber season, and the islanders send many boxes of them to the mainland," he answered, proud to be able to inform her of Greek life.

"Five o'clock, you said?" She looked at her watch, a large plain one with a white band that was part of her on-the-job uniform, even though she was dressed now in navy-blue slacks and a soft yellow sweater. "Two more hours. Are you tired? Do you want to lie down?"

Although the trip was short, she had booked a cabin so that he might nap if he needed rest.

"I am excited about seeing my home again, Nancy. I thought sometimes in the hospital that I would never see Korpas again. But even so, I think I had better sleep. I want to be wide awake when I see Kostas again."

Nancy supported his elbow, and he stood up slowly, careful of his footing on the gently rocking deck.

"It will be so good to speak with my brother again," he said, as if he had forgotten all about the hurt his brother had caused him. "And my little Kiki."

"Who is Kiki?" she asked, purposefully steering him away from thoughts of Kostas, afraid that the long-awaited reunion would fall short of his boyish expectations. "It sounds like the name of a dog or cat."

Niko didn't try to suppress his amusement, and his laughter pealed out. "Kiki is our servant," he said. "Her real name, Kiriaki, means Sunday. It is a funny name in English, isn't it? Because she has never married and has no brothers to take care of her, she lives in our house and takes very good care of us. She is very, very small and funny—you will see."

Cautiously, Nancy guided him toward the hatchway and up over the iron ledge that kept water from reaching the inner passageways. She was aware of how fragile he still was. One slip and he could fall and undo so much of the progress he had made. A broken bone would put an end to their therapy and send him back to bed for months.

They were in the carpeted passageway approaching the cabin door. "Does someone that small do all the work in your house?"

Nancy unlocked the door and pushed it open, making sure it caught in the latch so it wouldn't suddenly swing shut on him.

"No," he answered. "We have girls from the village who come in to clean. They work for Kiki, and Kiki works for us."

He pulled off his cap, and rich dark curls sprang up all over his head.

"Shall I help you with anything else, Niko, before you get into your bunk? Do you want anything from the suitcase?"

"No, I cannot keep you from your ocean. You must go back at once. You might miss seeing a wave." He stretched out on the bunk, and she pulled a gray blanket over him.

"Yes," she said, touching him gently on the cheek. "If I do, it will be the only wave in the whole Mediterranean today. I'll come in again in an hour, in case you need me."

"I will not need you. I will sleep like—what do you say in English? A rock?"

"No, silly, a log."

"Yes, a log. We have not this expression in Greek because we have so few trees. I will sleep like a log."

The next hour was bliss to Nancy. Without Niko, she was free to explore the boat from stem to stern and top to bottom, gawking at the colorful main deck, where chickens and people mingled in chaotic profusion. Women in black, with black kerchiefs on their heads, sat on bundles of their belongings crocheting and talking, with their black-stockinged legs stretched out in front of them. Children played among them, only stopping when a mother grabbed her child and popped a section of orange or some bread into his mouth. The men smoked and twisted "worry beads" around their fingers and shouted to one another over the din of the engine, which was especially loud down in deck class.

Nancy tried to understand their conversations, but all she could catch were the numbers and a few words she had learned from Niko. She hoped that by the time she left Greece she would be able to speak a few words herself.

Then, at last, it was four-thirty. The sun stood behind them, and the sky, although still bright, was more golden than blue. The island of Korpas appeared slowly off their port side. She ran to the cabin and found Niko awake. Within minutes he was beside her on the deck.

"There, that is the cove where we picnic," Niko cried, pointing out a notch in the cliffs. But they were soon past the spot, and the cliffs gave way to a rocky promontory.

"Niko! What is that?" Nancy cried in awe as a golden structure perched on the point of land came into view.

"That is the temple," said Niko. "If you want to know about it, you must ask Kostas. He knows everything."

She smiled wryly to herself as Niko once again elevated Kostas to heroic proportions. She was convinced he was wrong in his hero worship, yet she would never hurt him by letting him know what she believed.

"But there," the boy cried suddenly, pointing to a large white building on a hillside above a graceful bay, close to the temple, "that is my house."

What a view, thought Nancy, trying to take it in before the boat was past. "Why you must be able to see both the temple and the beach from your house!"

Immediately another point of land was rounded, and the ferry glided into a harbor, above which the small town rose, whitewashed houses gleaming in the clear air.

It wasn't just Nancy and Niko who were excited; the deck was charged with activity, and the concrete pier they were approaching seemed to be boiling over with people. As the boat drew closer and the shouts from the crew and those waiting on the pier grew almost equal in volume, Nancy saw that the curved harbor was ringed with outdoor cafés and that the whole town was watching their progress from either the dock or the tables at the water's edge.

But it soon became impossible to take in more impressions of the island with such a hubbub around her. Nancy's responsibility was to get Niko safely through the crowd of people clogging the passageways and the opening to the gangplank.

People were pushing and jostling to get on or off. Crates of chickens, huge bundles and plastic bags made the passageways difficult to get through. And worse, men in dusty fishing caps were moving in both directions on the narrow gangplank, carrying boxes of supplies from the mainland on their shoulders and returning for more. With her heart in her mouth, she took Niko firmly by the arm and began the steep descent down the gangplank.

Down they went, step by careful step over the raised struts, each an obstruction that could trip the boy and send him rolling down the incline to the concrete below. And suddenly, about halfway through the dangerous journey, she looked ahead of her to see a burly man dragging a heavy mailbag up toward them.

Nancy was terrified, certain that Niko would be knocked over. Instinctively, she stepped in front of the boy and faced the man, stretching her arms out to block him.

"Please, stop!" she cried. "This boy is injured. Give him room to get down safely."

The man, of course, didn't understand a word and began to shout at her in Greek. Nancy had just turned to Niko to ask him to translate when suddenly a deep male voice rang out over the din. Whatever it was he said in that imperious tone, it had an effect. Everyone in hearing distance stopped to listen. The fat man stopped shouting. He turned around and touched his cap respectfully.

Nancy looked past him down to the pier where she met the dark eyes of the man in the photograph. Immediately, she felt Niko stir behind her.

"*Yasou*, Kostas!" he cried with delight.

Instead of returning his brother's greeting, Kostas reprimanded him. "Do you want this man to go all the way back, Niko? You are closer. Return to the deck."

Nancy was shocked at Kostas's insensitive command.

"He's injured," she protested. "Why can't this man let Niko go down first?"

Kostas didn't even bother to answer her. "Do as I say, Niko!" he ordered the boy.

And Niko, eager to do his brother's bidding, began to turn around. Trembling with anger at the peremptory way Kostas had given his order, Nancy nevertheless had no choice but to help Niko back up the seemingly endless ramp. She anticipated another struggle to get down again. Hadn't Kostas the slightest consideration for his brother's safety? During the past weeks of preparation for the journey, when Kostas and the island were the constant topics of conversation, she had found herself hoping that Niko's obvious worship of his brother was justified. But now the man's unbelievable callousness in assuming that the lame boy had no rights over a perfectly healthy man clinched what she had sensed from that first disappointment—Kostas was an unfeeling selfish man.

The treacherous journey to the dock was negotiated at last, and they stood before Kostas on solid ground. He was at least a head taller than any of the villagers who surrounded him and he was dramatically different from them. It wasn't only his clothing, although Nancy had never seen such a well-cut pair of trousers and open-necked silk shirt except in the finest New York shops. He was, she realized, strikingly aristocratic looking, and there was a special vibrancy, a kind of magnetism, that expressed itself in the way he carried himself, his body as graceful and sleek as a panther. But his obvious strength was held in check, and the powerful voice well modulated. No wonder his orders commanded instant respect from the people on the dock.

Undaunted by the rebuff of his earlier greeting, Niko wholeheartedly embraced Kostas, kissing him on both cheeks in the European way, then turning to introduce Nancy.

Never had anyone looked at her the way Kostas Paradissis did. As the black eyes moved lingeringly over her body, she felt an unaccustomed flush stain her cheeks. A wave of heat rose in her, and despite herself, she dropped her eyes, only lifting her head when he put out a hand toward her.

With a shock, she realized that, although he shook her hand in a friendly-enough manner, there was no warmth in his eyes—only an aristocratic look of disdain. It was as if, after looking her over, he had decided she was not worthy of further consideration. Then he turned away abruptly to arrange for the luggage to be brought to the car.

The maroon Mercedes took them swiftly and relatively smoothly over the bumpy road that led west out of the town, and then they were snaking back and forth up the hill that separated the harbor from the Paradissis estate.

When they reached the top and began dipping down again, Nancy forgot Kostas's strange greeting and found herself looking at a golden carpet laid across the sea by the sun—a carpet, she thought, that extended directly to her, welcoming her to the most beautiful place she had ever seen. Silvery olive trees ran down the slopes toward the rocks at the water's edge, and to the right of the road, among low bushes, grazed a herd of goats with bells around their necks. Some women stooped among them, picking plants and stuffing them into their bulging aprons.

"What are the women doing?" asked Nancy, curious about every new sight to which she was being exposed.

"Those are herbs," Niko explained. "I do not know the names in English. You must ask Kostas," he laughed. "He knows everything about this island."

Nancy had never seen herbs growing in the wild. "What kind of herbs are they?" she heard herself asking, not knowing whether to address him as Kostas or Mr. Paradissis.

"Rosemary and oregano," Kostas said in his almost accent-free English, his eyes on the road ahead. "The women sell them in the shops to make a little money."

"But why should anyone go to the shops to buy them, if all they have to do is come up into the hills to gather what they want?" she asked.

"I cannot imagine who would do such a thing just to save a few *drachma*!" The sarcasm in his voice was unmistakable, chilling her enthusiasm. Her innocent question had not merited such an antagonistic response.

It was becoming uncomfortably evident that Kostas was angry about something, and she had the distinct impression that the something was her. She couldn't for the life of her imagine what she had done to annoy him, unless attempting to countermand his orders on the gangplank had put him in this black mood. Was this how it would be between them for the two months or more that Niko would need her before he was completely well? But perhaps he was always surly and unbending. If so, she would certainly see to it that their contact was limited. She wanted to enjoy her time here on the island with Niko, and that would be impossible if she were to be around the difficult Kostas. What a pity, she thought, that Kostas couldn't be friendlier, for he obviously had a greater command of English than Niko and knew infinitely more about the island.

The car swept down the mountainside and along an avenue of cypress trees leading to the house. At last Kostas pulled the car up before the front door and turned off the engine.

From the outside, the L-shaped house was large, but otherwise there was nothing in its architecture to distinguish it from many other modern houses she had seen in Piraeus. She had wondered at the plainness of the buildings they had passed on their taxi ride from the airport to the ferry. They had all looked the same—white with pastel-colored balconies and matching shutters across the windows. But now she discovered that the individuality of the Mediterranean home lay on the inside, for the residents to enjoy, not for all the world to see.

The walls were a foot thick to provide protection from the hot summer sun, and just inside the door in the spacious foyer stretched a floor of dark-green marble, looking like a glassy tidepool. Brass planters stood on either side of a white marble stairway, and ivy grew from them, long streamers twining up around the curving walls of the stairwell, adding grace to the austere entrance.

As she was taking it all in, a tiny woman in black, no more than four foot ten, came rushing up and grabbed Niko's face in both her hands.

"Niko, *pedi mou*!" she cried in a hoarse voice, tears springing to her eyes, "Niko, my child."

The way her hands pinched the flesh of his face, Nancy thought she might be hurting him. But no, Niko was ecstatic. He hugged her and kissed both her cheeks before saying to Nancy, with all the enthusiasm of boyish attachment, "Here is Kiki. Here is my Sunday."

"How do you do," said Nancy, putting out her hand, and at once it was clasped by ten tiny but strong fingers and pumped up and down vigorously. "You make Niko well. You very fine person," Kiki said, pumping away, her black eyes sparkling.

"That will do, Kiki," Kostas interrupted curtly. "Please take these valises to her room."

Nancy looked at her heavy suitcases and back at the tiny woman. "Oh, no, let me take them," she said.

But Kiki had already lifted them and was halfway across the floor. Nancy, unaccustomed to having others do things for her, stood watching uncomfortably, fighting the urge to run and take them herself. Kostas, seeing her expression, resolved her difficulty.

"Our peasant women are strong, like donkeys," he said.

And with that unflattering observation, he suggested in a voice that brooked no contradiction that she might like to rest before the evening meal.

Kiki led her to a high-ceilinged, whitewashed room, again needing little decoration beyond the pink marble floor. The windows and what appeared to be a door to the outside were shuttered.

Kiki had already opened a suitcase and was hanging Nancy's dresses in an antique armoire.

"No, Kiki, you must let me do that," she said, determined not to adopt Kostas's cavalier attitude toward his servant.

Kiki flashed a smile at her and went back to her work. "You let Kiki work, Despinis Nancy. Your strength must be for Niko."

Nancy had no choice but to give in, she realized, but she told Kiki she needn't call her *Despinis*—Miss—every time she addressed her. After all, Nancy called the little woman only Kiki!

When the unpacking was done, Kiki closed the suitcase with a click, then went over to the shuttered door.

"Niko was hurt very bad," she explained somberly, shaking her head with emotion. With both hands she took a cord on the side of the door and pulled. The window shutter began to rattle up a few inches. "Kostas Paradissis thought Niko would not walk again, not swim, not fish and hunt. Never become a man."

She pulled again, harder, and the shutter went up some more. "Kiki prayed, went to the church and prayed Niko get well."

The light in the room was becoming more and more brilliant, and already Nancy could see the value of the thick walls and uncarpeted marble floors as the heat began to pour in from outside.

"And it was a miracle. Niko is well, with your help."

"And Dr. Davies's help, Kiki," said Nancy, coming to her side just as the shutter reached the top of the French window. "Oh," she breathed as she caught her first glimpse of the view across the wide veranda to the golden sea. Kiki opened the glass double doors, and Nancy stepped out onto the hot concrete.

"Kiki, do you realize you have the Aegean in your backyard?"

She was so thrilled at the discovery that she did not think to speak softly. Her voice echoed against the concrete and rang against the house. A chair scraped overhead, and she looked up. There was a balcony above that ran the width of the second floor.

"We have the sunset in our garden, as well," came Kostas's voice, deep and well modulated from above. "Walk around to the side, Miss Spaulding, and you will see what I mean."

Nancy obeyed the disembodied voice, taking a few steps around the west corner of the house. Here the veranda was narrow and fell away to a steep hillside dark with cypress trees. Beyond the trees the orange sun sank toward the horizon, touching with red and gold the sky around it and the water and the startling pillars of the ruined temple she had seen from the boat.

"Aphrodite's temple," came Kostas's voice again, as if he knew the question she was about to ask.

Nothing Niko had ever said to her about the island had prepared her for such a scene. It was grander than any picture could have been. The air was clearer, the light bolder and the silence deeper than anything she could have imagined.

She heard another movement above, and then a door opened and closed. Behind her, Kiki sighed and went in. Nancy was left alone with the sun that was dipping its brilliant flame into the wine-dark sea.

The light evening meal was served in a vine-covered arbor nestled in an ell of the house. For the first time, as

Nancy sipped pungent local wine and ate the excellent mushroom *omeletta* Kiki had put before her with a side dish of fried eggplant, she felt her anxiety relax about Niko's well-being during his first days out of the hospital. Now that he was safely with his family again, there was nothing more to fear, and she began to realize that despite the therapy still necessary to his weak muscles, this would really be a vacation for her. With his capable father and Kiki present, Niko would not have to rely on her for constant care. She would have plenty of time to explore the island and the town, to lie in the sun, to do some jogging and best of all, to swim.

Then, as she speared a cucumber from among the tomatoes and olives in the salad, she realized she had not included Kostas among those who would care for Niko. Either she was terribly mistaken or Kostas was the sort of man who felt it beneath him to care for those weaker than himself. She glanced across the table at him, and her eyes met his for the second time that day. What did it mean, this dark fiery look? She dropped her eyes immediately, as though she would be burned. His expression seemed almost threatening.

At least Antonis Paradissis was capable of bending. He was quite transformed from the authoritarian man she had met in New York. Here, in the light of a single electric bulb that threw huge shadows of grape leaves against the white wall, he was expansive and jovial, making Nancy and the boy laugh. Only Kostas did not join in their lighthearted banter, but kept bringing the conversation to business, as if to exclude her and Niko.

"You will see, father," he was saying with the controlled intensity he seemed to bring to everything he did, "when the plant in Saloniki is in operation, we will be able to double the volume. Shipping from Germany is slow and costly. We will import the parts now and let our own people assemble them. Within ten years, I can guarantee that we will be manufacturing everything ourselves. It is the future, father."

"You must forgive my son," Antonis said, turning to Nancy. "He has, as you say, a bee in his bonnet. Now that he has taken over the business from me, he thinks he can single-handedly begin an industrial revolution in Greece. I am older and more conservative than he. I argue with him about taking such risks with what I have spent a lifetime building, but he is better educated than I. He thinks he can conquer the world like Alexander the Great. Perhaps he is right."

How much power and money could Kostas want, Nancy found herself wondering, swallowing the last of her wine as she looked at the two men and the boy. They obviously were an extremely wealthy family. When she had mentioned the name Paradissis to her brother-in-law, Burt's eyes had widened and he had told her it was one of the best-known names in that part of the world. Burt's company had done business with them, so he knew they were responsible for importing a huge quantity of American-made business machines to Greece. Besides that, Burt had informed her, the Paradissis Company imported other items, mainly recreational equipment and farm machinery from Germany. If Kostas had taken over most of the running of the business from his father, then he wielded tremendous power and must have considerable wealth at his command. Why was it necessary to build an ever-greater empire?

Recalling the Mercedes and the well-cut clothes, Nancy answered her own question. With his evident love of fine and expensive things, Kostas might not be satisfied until the family fortune was tripled. He was probably one of those driving ambitious tycoons with no room in his life for personal involvement or warmth, the exact antithesis of everything she admired in a man.

"Nancy, it is a full moon," Niko said when the meal was over. "Come with me to see the temple. They say the goddess sometimes comes there on nights like this."

"And will Aphrodite pick you up when you fall from the cliff, Niko?" Kostas asked sarcastically.

Nancy, who had risen and walked toward the veranda, turned quickly to the boy, expecting to see Niko's face crestfallen and his spirits crushed by his brother's cutting words. But she was surprised to find the smile still there and mischief in his olive eyes.

"Then you will have to go instead, Kostas," he sang out cheerfully, "for Nancy must see the temple. But be careful that *she* does not fall. I need her for swimming tomorrow."

Nancy was dismayed at the prospect of going anywhere with Kostas. "No, Niko," she said. "I will wait for you. When you are stronger, we'll go together."

But Kostas waved her objections aside. "I shall be pleased to show you the temple," he said politely, if stiffly, she thought. "Niko is right. It is a perfect night. Will you excuse us, father?"

She had no choice but to go with him, it seemed, for Niko would not let her refuse. She walked with Kostas out of the arbor and across the veranda, following him through the fragrant darkness as he led the way along a narrow path.

When they were out of earshot of the boy and his father, she said, "Why did you say such an unkind thing to Niko?"

She would never have dared to reprove him under ordinary circumstances, but it was her patient he had mistreated, and she felt that it was her duty to make Kostas understand that the still delicate medical condition of his brother required patience and consideration.

"We do not believe in coddling the sick," Kostas answered without turning around. "Unlike you Americans, we do not wish to encourage weakness."

They were out of sight of the lighted area and the full moon hung above them, silver in a velvet sky. The tranquil scene accentuated the harshness of his tone as they passed through the cypresses and along the point of land toward the temple.

"But surely you can be kind," she said to his unyielding back. "Kindness is not weakness."

Again he answered her without stopping or even turning. "In ancient times, crippled children were exposed to the elements and left to die. We are more humane than that now. But a man still needs to be strong, and Niko will soon be a man."

She couldn't think of a response. Kostas was so sure of himself. He obviously expected no contradiction to his unfeeling remark. In his own mind he knew best, and she, although Niko's nurse and closer to the child during these past few months than he had been, was not entitled to any opinion at all. It seemed to her they were worlds apart. She had dedicated her life to caring for the weak and infirm, and Kostas appeared to have nothing but contempt for those less than perfect.

How was she to speak to such a man, get him to understand Niko's needs during this crisis in his life? If she told him how the boy had waited eagerly for his letters and how he read every word again and again, would Kostas see how important it was to be kind to his brother?

He moved on before her, black against the dazzling moon, and she found herself looking closely at his dark form. He was not tall by American standards, but taller than most Mediterranean men. His chest and shoulders were broad and powerful looking, his legs thick and strong. He was no slim young statue like the *Chariot Boy* in the museum at Delphi. Greek stock had changed since classical times, mixed with the darker North Africans. His body was not made for beauty alone, but for use, and he carried that body in such a way that there was no mistaking the impression that he knew its power and kept it in perfect condition, at his full command.

He let her catch up with him, taking her arm to assist her down a sharp incline. She felt her own frailty in this gesture. Self-sufficient as she liked to think of herself, she enjoyed the momentary sense of her own femininity.

Then suddenly they were down among the ruined pillars, and she forgot everything else. A faint breeze from the sea stirred the curls around her face. The temple rose white and faintly sinister above her, and beneath her sandaled feet stretched the same alabaster slabs on which priestesses had stood, serving Aphrodite, goddess of love, more than two millenia ago.

"It's beautiful. It's...eternal," she whispered, unashamed of a romantic statement she would never have made in daylight. "I can almost believe that the Greek gods exist in a place like this."

She felt him looking at her and turned to see a faint smile on his moonlit face.

"I feel that, too," he said, his voice suddenly gentle.

The moon touched with silver the lock of black hair that fell down over his forehead, and he looked boyish and young. She saw a stronger resemblance to Niko in the well-shaped nose, generous mouth and large deep-set eyes. Something stirred within her. He really was the most attractive man she'd ever seen, she thought as they stood listening to the lapping of waves at the base of the cliff. Then the elusive emotion died as quickly as it had flared.

"Niko was right, Mr. Paradissis," she said politely. "The temple is magnificent."

Kostas inclined his head slightly, and it was impossible to read the expression in his eyes. "It is a very special place, is it not? The sight of this temple banishes all black thoughts. Yes, there is something eternal here—you are right. But I am uncomfortable being called Mr. Paradissis," he said in a faintly mocking tone. "My name is Kostas."

He took a step toward her, and his hands reached out. She remembered the way he had looked at her on the dock. Her heart pounding, she stepped away from him to avoid what she feared would be an embrace.

To her surprise, Kostas began to laugh. "What are you afraid of?" he asked, taking her arm and turning her firmly around toward the path. "Did you think I would offer you as a sacrifice? I told you I was civilized. I am merely trying to guide you back. It is late, and I must finish some business."

Nancy lifted a hand to her mouth. "I'm sorry, Mr...Kostas," she stammered, rigid with embarrassment. "I'm not used to all this—the temple and the wine have both gone to my head."

"And you are not used to me, either, I think," he continued with a charming smile. "You must be sure not to let *me* go to your head."

Alone in her room, where Kiki had closed the shutters and turned back the handwoven, red-and-white bedspread, she began to think about Kostas's strange words. At the time, they had made her feel uncomfortable. She had taken the remark as just another sign of his conceit. But the more she thought about it, the more perplexed she became. She sensed a deeper meaning behind his apparently light last comment than she first had suspected. Why, she wondered, should he feel it necessary to warn her? An involvement with Kostas was the furthest thing from her mind.

CHAPTER THREE

NANCY AWOKE unable to resist pulling open the shutters to gaze out at the incomparable view of the sea and beach below. Even after a week on Korpas, the sheer physical beauty of the island—the cypress-clad slopes, the cloudless skies and the crystal waters—still worked its spell. It would be difficult to return to city life after her work in Korpas was done, she knew.

No wonder Niko had missed his home so sorely, she thought one morning as she slipped into a pair of shorts and a T-shirt to go for her usual brisk run on the beach. The fresh morning breeze played with her short hair and caressed her face, while the firm sand under her feet and the occasional lapping of waves around her trim ankles filled her with exuberance. She returned to the house feeling full of life and vitality. Then she bathed and dressed to join Niko for a light breakfast of thick, sweet Turkish coffee and freshly baked crescent rolls.

In only a week, the boy had begun to blossom, and the hospital pallor was giving way to a healthy glow.

Yes, Nancy thought, everything on Korpas would be perfect—if it were not for Kostas. His strange remark at the temple had gone unexplained and was all the more puzzling because he had once again become aloof, showing no signs of the charm she had glimpsed then. At suppertime he would politely inquire after her health, ask her one or two dutiful questions in an indifferent tone of voice, and then switch to business conversation with his father.

However once or twice during her swimming sessions with Niko, she had happened to glance up at the house only to see Kostas standing on his balcony, leaning against the railing looking down at them. Although it was too far away to be sure, she felt somehow certain he was looking at them in disapproval. It was clear to her that for some unfathomable reason Kostas objected to her. And this had a disturbing effect on her. She wondered how two brothers could be so different—Niko, so sweet and open and full of affection, and Kostas, the personification of arrogant disdain.

"Nancy, you look different today," Niko commented as she came onto the veranda.

"You mean because I'm wearing a dress?" She had put on a crisp white sundress printed with yellow sunflowers.

He tossed his head back in the wordless Greek gesture for "no," and his eyes shone. "Not only your clothing. I think your face has changed since you came here. You look very beautiful. But of course you were always beautiful," he added quickly.

"You are a charmer," Nancy laughed, sitting beside him at the table and helping herself to a croissant stuffed with nuts and cinnamon. "I dressed up because I thought I would walk into town before our exercises today."

He frowned. "But it is very hot. You must go early in the morning with Kiki when she markets. Or perhaps Kostas will take you in the car."

"I'll go with Kiki another time," she answered firmly, sure that Kostas would be no more delighted by Niko's suggestion than she was. "But this morning I intend to go by myself. You forget, Niko, for me this will be an adventure. Besides, I'm all out of suntan lotion and need some more."

The road leading from the house was narrow and steep, but afforded such a magnificent view of the sparkling sea and terraced land that she was at first oblivious to everything but the beauty around her. As the road turned and dipped toward the town, she passed women carrying tins of olive oil or baskets of fruit and vegetables. Nancy was aware of their frank and curious stares. Korpas was not used to foreigners, she realized.

She walked for nearly a mile, and although it was still early, the sun had become blazing hot. Her sandals, comfortable for city walking, were not suited to the unpaved road, and each pebble left its imprint on the soles of her feet. Next time, she told herself, beginning to feel ridiculous, she would wear tennis shoes, as well as a sun hat against the heat. Just as she was thinking this, she heard the sound of a speeding car. She turned around to see Kostas's maroon Mercedes heading toward her. The car pulled alongside and stopped.

When Kostas reached across the seat and opened the passenger door for her, her first impulse was to get in, for the air-conditioned, luxurious automobile was tempting. As she moved toward the car, however, Kostas began to chastise her.

"It is much too long a walk in the heat," he said. "You should have known better, especially after Niko warned you."

She looked at him in surprise. His skin was coppery against the pale blue of his open-necked sports shirt, his thick dark hair was ruffled from the breeze. Nancy, the professional, who was always reasonable about health and safety, recognized the truth in his words and knew she was better off in the car than outside it. But Nancy, the woman, had her own contradictory reactions. How dare he speak to her as if she were a willful child needing a scolding! She pulled away from the door, bristling with annoyance.

"Thank you, but I prefer to walk."

His eyes swept over her, taking note of her bare head and sandaled feet.

"This is not Manhattan," he replied. "You have at least three more miles and the road does not improve. You will have sunstroke."

"The heat doesn't bother me," she countered, refusing to be humiliated by his patronizing manner. "I'm quite capable of walking three miles."

Kostas clicked his tongue in impatience, and his fingers drummed on the steering wheel. He looked as if he were barely controlling his temper. "I am a busy man. I do not have all morning to waste. Get in."

Did he think that everyone must do exactly as he ordered? She felt determined, now, to show him that she would not be bullied.

"Then why bother coming after me?" she retorted. "You're free to go home and put your time to better use."

"If you become ill with sunstroke," he responded in a tone that was barely civil, "then much more of my time will be taken. Stop your foolishness and get in."

"I won't become ill. I can take care of myself," she said, slamming the car door shut.

The impatience on his face turned, for a brief instant, to anger. Then with a careless shrug of his powerful shoulders, he turned the car around.

Nancy felt a momentary surge of elation at her "victory" as he sped back toward the house in a cloud of dust. She had shown him she had a mind of her own. But the momentary triumph faded when she recalled the way he had looked at her, his penetrating eyes seeing through her. She had put on a show of defiance, she realized, but it was a show only. Actually, she had been intimidated by him. He was so powerful and so sure of himself. She had never felt weak before or particularly vulnerable. Why did he affect her this way?

Resolving not to let such thoughts spoil her morning, Nancy turned her attention back to the three-mile walk facing her. As if to spite Kostas, she survived the heat and the rough stones remarkably well and at last reached the town.

The residential part of the town was like a scene from another century, she thought, as she wandered leisurely in and out of narrow side streets. Old women in black, with gnarled, sun-darkened faces sat working lace or crocheting on straw-matted chairs in doorways.

"Kalimera," she said politely when she passed them. She had learned the phrase meaning good-morning from Niko.

The women answered her greeting enthusiastically, their eyes smiling at her, their fingers never missing a stitch.

She greeted everyone she met, and as a result several women invited her for coffee, and although she politely refused, each had a smile and a good word in response. Dr. Davies had been right, she thought, for never had she met friendlier people. Even the dusty men on donkey-back, who came in from the hills carrying loads of vegetables or twigs, put their hands to their caps and answered her now confident good-morning.

The whole town was no larger than five Manhattan city blocks, she realized with amusement, recalling the huge steel and concrete city she had only just left. The cobblestoned market street was lined on both sides with small shops. She passed butchers with carcasses hanging in windows from metal hooks and a bakery where the pungent aroma of freshly baked bread floated out to her. There were shops that displayed trays of honey-drenched pastries and small *tavernas* from which came the rich sound of male voices and bouzouki music. In the main square, alongside the harbor, she viewed a half dozen or so cafés, where groups of idle young men dressed in up-to-the-minute European fashions sat at small wooden tables engrossed in their games of *tavli*.

Finally she paused in front of a small shop with windows crammed with books, stationery and gift items. Perhaps she could buy a postcard here so she could show Jan exactly where she was.

She entered to find the one room crammed with every kind of writing material: the usual paper, pencils and erasers; Greek-language books and newspapers; greeting cards and even comic books. Nancy peered into the display case, trying to figure out the equivalence of the prices written in drachmas.

"I've been hoping you'd come in," a voice with a strong British accent cried out as she was reaching for a postcard that showed the temple at sunset. "You're the American, aren't you?"

Startled, Nancy turned to see a young red-haired woman staring at her with undisguised curiosity, a friendly smile lighting her freckled face.

"I'm Barbara Savalos," the woman said, extending her hand. "We—my husband, Panos, and I—own this shop."

Nancy took the woman's hand, surprised and pleased to find someone about her age who spoke English. "Yes, I'm Nancy Spaulding. But how did you know who I was?"

Barbara's laugh was good-natured. "Everyone in Korpas knows everything about everyone. You'll find how true that is if you stay any length of time, which I hope you will. We've known that an American was coming back with Niko, and then Panos spotted you when you arrived on the ferry."

Barbara stood back, her arms folded over her chest and appraised Nancy. "I must say for once my dear husband did not exaggerate. He said you were very pretty!"

Nancy smiled self-consciously, not sure what to say.

"I hope I'm not offending you," Barbara went on. "I've so been looking forward to meeting you. But you must have come in for something other than conversation, although I'd like nothing better than to talk."

Nancy picked out a few more postcards and added to her purchase an English detective story that Barbara produced from under a pile of Greek sports magazines.

"If you aren't in too great a hurry," Barbara said after wrapping Nancy's parcel in brown paper and tying it with twine, "let me take you to the café for a few minutes. We can have a cool drink and get to know each other. There's little business today, and if anybody really needs me, they'll know where to find me. It's a small town, as I said."

After putting a chair in the doorway to indicate that she was closed and would return soon, Barbara companionably slipped an arm through Nancy's and led her across the square to a small café.

The thick rich smell of Turkish coffee mingled with the salt breeze from the sea. They sat down at an aluminum table under the striped awning. A portly middle-aged waiter came to take their order, and after speaking a few words to him in Greek, Barbara turned to introduce Nancy.

"Nancy, this is Dimitri. Dimitri, meet Nancy Spaulding."

The waiter's face broke into a smile. He bobbed his head at her as if she were his oldest and dearest friend. Soon she and Barbara were sipping cool refreshing glasses of fruit juice and chatting amiably.

"Your Greek sounds good," Nancy observed enviously. "How long have you lived here?"

"Oh dear, don't get me started or you'll have my whole life story," Barbara answered. "I came here nearly five years ago, on holiday from my job in London. Who would think when I chose this remote island that it would change my life? Would you believe I met Panos the first day I was here!" She laughed, her blue eyes sparkling with pleasure at the recollection. "Here at this café, in fact! And after two days, I knew I would never leave! Greek men do have a way about them, as I'm sure you've discovered."

Catching a curious note in her voice, Nancy looked up to see unabashed amusement in the other woman's eyes.

"I'm referring to Kostas, of course!" Barbara exclaimed. "He is quite the charmer."

"I haven't noticed that particular quality," Nancy remarked, feeling a flush creep into her cheeks.

"Ah ha!" Barbara laughed again. "But you must admit that he *is* extremely handsome and intelligent."

"Yes, I'll concede that," Nancy replied, returning the other girl's irresistible smile. And arrogant, she thought, remembering the way he had tried to order her into the car.

"It should be very interesting," Barbara mused, twirling her straw in her glass. "Now that I've seen you . . ."

"I don't understand…." Something in the woman's tone made Nancy feel uncomfortable.

Barbara patted her arm. "Never mind, darling. I'm just an incurable romantic. But I'm so glad you turned out to be young. I was sure if Kostas had his way, Niko would have had a seventy-five-year-old Greek woman for a therapist!"

"What do you mean?" Nancy asked, her curiosity aroused.

"Oh dear." Barbara laughed in embarrassment. "Panos says I talk too much. Now, put away your purse. This is my treat."

After Barbara had paid Dimitri for the drinks, they walked back together across the square. In front of the shop Barbara turned to her.

"Nancy, I do hope we'll be friends. You and Panos will like each other, I'm sure. You must come to supper one evening soon."

"That would be wonderful," said Nancy with delight.

"Then let's say Friday, if you're free."

Glowing with the pleasure of new friendship and the prospect of an evening out, Nancy took a taxi back. She returned in time for an hour's work with Niko on leg and back exercises in the small study off the entrance hall that Niko's father had converted into a therapy room. There was no sign of Kostas, for which she was grateful.

Late that afternoon, Nancy went to the beach for a run. After finishing, she walked in the shallow water, enjoying the cool wavelets swirling around her ankles. Impulsively, she knelt down, and scooping water in her cupped hands, splashed it over her flushed face, where it dripped down over her cotton shirt and shorts. Shaking her head like a puppy, she started up the path to the veranda and found Kostas standing near the top watching her.

A flash of annoyance went through her. She didn't want another encounter with him today, especially now, with her water-spotted clothing and hair that was rapidly going frizzy. As always, Kostas was impeccably dressed in white pants and a navy-blue short-sleeved silk shirt, open at the throat. He was staring at her bare legs and feet as she approached.

"I didn't die of sunstroke," she said brashly.

He inclined his head slightly toward her as she drew closer, and his eyes seemed to mock her as they roamed over her slim legs and body.

Nancy felt her color deepen, aware of his dark eyes on her as she brushed by him on her way to the veranda.

"So I see. You seem to be always running or swimming or working. You are like a perpetual-motion machine. I wonder, do you never wind down?"

So he *had* been watching her daily activities, Nancy thought angrily, feeling as though her privacy had been invaded.

"I didn't expect to have an audience, Mr. Paradissis," she retorted coolly, turning to face him. "Had I known you'd be watching me this afternoon, I would have dressed for the occasion."

Kostas laughed, and his coffee-colored eyes again moved insolently over her body, slowly this time. Nancy could see the pulse beating in the hollow of his throat.

"I see no need for a change. Your present attire suits you quite well. The natural all-American girl."

Nancy met his gaze evenly. "You seem to know a lot about American girls."

Kostas's face darkened. "I was educated in your country. My engineering degree is from the University of California. While there, I had much occasion to know American women." His lips curled, showing his even white teeth. "Too much," he added with a curiously bitter emphasis.

Nancy was surprised to learn that he was an engineer. Somehow she had thought of him simply as a rich man's son who had stepped into command of the family business. Of course, she realized his English was too good for him not to have spent some time in England or the States.

"American girls are an interesting breed." Kostas's voice shifted and took on a bantering tone as she turned and continued up the stony path, aware—all too aware—that he followed her.

She was grateful that he was unable to see her flaming face. He made American girls sound like a species of insect, and she longed to hurl an insult at him in return.

"Most of my countrymen find American woman too unfeminine," he went on lightly. "They appear to be so independent, compared to Greek women, but it is only a matter of appearances. Americans are good at appearances."

Nancy began to answer, to refute his generalizations, but in turning she stumbled on a small rock. She fell back and was stopped by Kostas's arm, which shot out and caught her around the waist. Despite herself, she gasped at the physical contact, and as he continued to hold her a few seconds longer than was necessary, she became acutely aware of the strength of muscle and bone underneath the cool silk.

Pulling herself upright, she turned from him at once and made a rush toward the veranda.

Kostas's triumphant laugh rang out in the still air. "The American woman," he said. "She would prefer to walk three miles in the heat rather than accept a ride, and all to assert her so-called independence! Tell me, Nancy, wouldn't it be easier to accept the help that's offered to you? Why do you run away?"

Nancy turned and glared at him. "I can take care of myself very well, thank you."

"Of course," Kostas said with mock sincerity. "Only, I might suggest you wear shoes on these paths."

Nancy glanced down at her sandy bare feet.

"These paths are not easily negotiable, and you might have hurt your ankle. Also, there are scorpions here. You will not enjoy the experience of stepping on one, I assure you."

They had reached the house, and Nancy, burning with resentment at his supercilious tone, was eager to escape through the French doors into her room. But before she could do that, Kostas took her arm and stopped her progress. His fingers closed tightly around her wrist.

"I did not come to spy on you, Nancy," he said, "but to tell you that my father and I must go to Athens tomorrow morning. My father will remain there for some time, but I will return in several days. Until then, you are essentially in charge."

His face became serious, and Nancy was surprised at the difference in his appearance when the arrogant expression disappeared. He seemed suddenly more human. More like Niko.

"Should any problem arise," he continued gravely, "please telephone me at once. I rely on your good judgment." He released her wrist and took a card from his shirt pocket.

"I don't anticipate any problems with Niko. He's doing very well," she said, taking the card and looking down at it, unwilling to let him see her pleasure at his unexpected confidence in her.

A change crept into Kostas's voice. "No doubt," he said dryly.

"And should any problems come up," she added, stung by his change of tone, "I'd naturally telephone your father."

"I said to call *me*, Miss Spaulding! My father is an old man, and he has, in addition, a weak heart. I am the one to be contacted, at the number on the card. Do you understand?"

Nancy colored. "As you like. Excuse me."

Aware of his eyes on her, she strode swiftly through the door and let the shutter slide shut.

CHAPTER FOUR

KIKI CAME OUT of the kitchen door with her apron on from washing the dishes and asked in halting English if Nancy would like something.

Nancy had been sitting in the shady arbor while Niko napped, trying to write to her sister. But after the first line she had found herself unable to concentrate. She kept feeling the grip of Kostas's strong hand on her wrist the previous afternoon, and the intimate way his bold eyes had scrutinized her body as she had climbed the path. He was truly insufferable, she thought, remembering his words to her and the abrupt way he had ordered her to telephone him, as if she were his servant. Yet now that he was gone, the house seemed forlorn. Surely it was a relief to know that he was away, no longer able to find fault with her. She did not understand why she felt so oddly restless and discontented.

"No, Kiki," she answered, shaking herself out of her apathy. "I don't need a thing."

She hadn't the heart to make more work for Kiki, who must be dying for her daily nap. But the little servant wasn't satisfied with this answer. She returned to the kitchen and came back a minute later with a cup of coffee on a tray, along with a glass of water and a teaspoonful of what looked like jelly.

"This is *glyko*, to make you feel sweet," said Kiki, telling her to take the Greek confection on her tongue and wash it down with water.

"Do I look like I need sweetening?" Nancy asked.

"Today, yes. You have a very long face. Also, you must get a little bit fat or no man will want to marry you."

"But American men don't want fat wives," protested Nancy, nevertheless sliding the jelly into her mouth. It was so sweet she was afraid she would choke, and she took the cold water gratefully.

"You, Nancy, must marry a Greek man, stay in Greece. If Kiki had a boy, she would give him to you."

"Thank you, Kiki," Nancy laughed. "I wish I could stay here in Greece forever and ever. But I don't want to marry just to do that."

"You wait too long, you become old lady like Kiki. You must find good Greek man, marry right away. *Etsi einai zoe!* That is life!"

"But I have my career, Kiki. I'm happy with my work, helping boys like Niko."

Kiki didn't answer. Giving her a keen look, she picked up the tray and headed back to the kitchen door.

"Kiki knows best, you will see," she said, and went inside.

Nancy returned to her letter writing, but before she had finished a sentence, the telephone's ring startled her. Soon she heard the hurried patter of Kiki's little feet coming back toward her.

"Nancy, please. For you on the *telefono*."

Nancy's heart lurched in alarm. Her first thought was that there might be trouble at home. She followed Kiki to the library and picked up the receiver to hear Kostas's deep voice.

"I am sorry to disturb you," he said brusquely.

Nancy felt immediate relief. "Kostas, I'm so glad it's you," she said breathlessly.

"Oh?" Kostas's voice lost its edge. "Why is that?"

"I was afraid it was my sister calling to say something was wrong at home," she explained hastily, unnerved by his apparent misinterpretation of her enthusiastic response.

"Yes, naturally," he said quickly. Once more he became businesslike. "Please, would you be so good as to do a favor for me?"

"Of course."

"I have forgotten a very important letter on the desk in my room. It is from an electronics firm in Texas. As Kiki cannot read English, I must ask your help. Would you please fetch it and read it to me? I will wait."

She put the receiver down and for the first time climbed the marble stairs to his room. Kostas occupied half of the upper floor and his father the other half. Kostas's room was handsomely decorated in blue, with lovely woven curtains and a royal-blue handmade bedspread. It was a masculine room, with a rifle and various enlargements of aerial photographs on the walls. Every window offered a splendid view of sea or cypress trees or rugged hills.

Although in the room on his orders and with his knowledge, Nancy had the uneasy sensation of having trespassed where she did not belong. Their relationship was far too impersonal for her to be comfortable here among his intimate possessions. She felt as though Kostas himself were present, and she even thought she could smell the aftershave lotion he wore, a spicy fresh scent.

On the desk was the letter he had described, with its American stamp. As she picked it up, her eyes fell on a large color photograph in a brown leather frame. There was Kostas standing on the polished deck of a yacht, one arm intimately draped over the naked shoulders of a shapely, bikini-clad young woman. She was long-legged and raven-haired, a seductive smile on her perfect oval face.

Nancy felt her breath catch in her throat, but she had no time to study the picture with Kostas waiting on the phone. Clutching the letter, she hurried back to the library where she read him the specifications and figures he asked for.

After he hung up, Nancy returned to the arbor. A slight breeze had come up, fanning the grape leaves above her head. The table was dappled in sunlight, and the sound of cicadas shrilled from the cypress trees in the drive. She picked up her pen once more but still could not write. Her mind was on the photograph. Who was the young woman, she wondered. Of course, it was natural for Kostas to have women friends. Despite his arrogance, he was undeniably handsome and magnetic.

Did he show a different side to this woman, she wondered, than the aloof and imperious personality she had come to know? His attitude toward her had been anything but charming, yet Barbara seemed to be taken by his "charm." Worse, he continued to exhibit an unsympathetic stand toward Niko's health. Whenever she helped the child in some way, no matter how trivial, even suggesting to him that he wear a sweater on a cool evening, an unmistakable flash of annoyance would flicker over Kostas's face. Why this should be she didn't know. Yet Niko himself seemed not to notice or care and remained as affectionate toward his brother as always.

She looked down at the page in front of her. "Dearest Jan," she had written. Aside from the date, and the beginning of one sentence, the rest of the page was blank.

She crumpled up the sheet in disgust. She was spending too much time thinking about Kostas Paradissis and not enough on the important daily tasks before her. Kostas was not her concern. Niko and her sister were.

Yet even as she chastised herself and took out a fresh piece of paper, her mind moved uncontrollably back to the way Kostas's strong arm had caught her as she had stumbled on the path.

NIKO WAS UNUSUALLY QUIET that evening. When Nancy set up the checkers after Kiki had cleared the supper table, he lost two games in a row to her.

"Niko, you're losing your touch," Nancy chided. "Why don't you teach me one of your Greek games? That should be more interesting."

He shrugged his slender shoulders. "I do not feel like playing tonight. I will teach you tomorrow."

"I'm sure you miss your father and brother, but Niko, we'll have so much fun together while they're away that the days will pass very quickly."

Niko shook his dark head slowly, and when he looked up at her there was sadness in his large eyes.

"You are a very dear friend, Nancy," he said, "to try to make me happy. But in this matter there is nothing you can do, because this trip, I believe, will bring something special, something not pleasant to me."

"And what could that be?" she asked, gathering up the checkers.

"Kostas and papa are arranging for Kostas's marriage."

Nancy felt her heart give a sudden lurch.

"It was arranged some time ago that Kostas will marry Loukia Kassandras," he said. "It is a contract made between the two families in the old-fashioned way. When I had my accident, they postponed their engagement. But now I have come home and am almost well, I am certain they will begin to make their plans."

Nancy carefully put the checkers back into the box, hiding her fingertips, which had begun to tremble just a little.

"But if he's going to marry her, Niko, then Kostas must love her. You should be happy for him, not sad."

"But you do not know her!" Niko said with unusual vehemence. "Her family has much, much money, and my father is good friends with her father. But she is not a good woman, Nancy. I know this. On the outside Loukia is very beautiful, yes. But inside she is selfish and mean, and she does not like me at all."

"Niko, how could anyone not like you? I'm sure it's not so."

"She never speaks to me, except when my father or Kostas are around. And when Kostas and Loukia are married, she will live here all the time, and I will never be happy on my island again."

"Niko, Niko," she said, taking his hands in hers. "I'm sure things will work out. You know, things are seldom as bad as we think. When my parents died, I was only a year older than you, and I thought it was the end of the world. Of course, it was a great tragedy, and I still miss them, but life goes on. I went to school and found a career I enjoyed, and I met you—and here I am on this wonderful island!"

Niko smiled. "You are the best friend I ever had, Nancy, but you can be wrong, too. Some things will never work out for the best. I will never learn to like Loukia."

JUST BEFORE GOING to bed, Nancy stood at her bedroom window and watched the moonlight glimmering on the water. Her short yellow nightgown stirred in the breeze. But the music of the waves did not soothe her as it usually did. She was not sure what oppressed her this evening. Perhaps it was just sympathy for Niko's unhappiness.

Change was difficult for adolescents, she knew, and she felt sorry for him. Nevertheless, she was certain that his fears were unjustified. Most likely he imagined this Loukia to be indifferent because he was too sensitive, and because he was afraid he would lose his brother's affection, such as it was.

But what if he were right and Loukia was selfish and indifferent? Then she and Kostas deserve each other, Nancy told herself fiercely, closing the shutters with a bang and climbing into bed.

"American women," Kostas had said to her. "So independent as compared with Greek women. But it is only a matter of appearance."

That's what Niko says about Loukia, she thought, turning on her side and pulling the sheet over her shoulder—that she's beautiful on the outside only. Why then, with his attitude, would Kostas want to marry her? Could a man like Kostas be so easily deceived?

Then, as she began to drift off to sleep, the memory of his arm around her waist as they returned from the beach came to her sharply with something like pain, and she pulled the pillow over her head to drive away the sudden sense of loss that welled up in her.

ALONE IN THE CLEAR WATER of the bay, Nancy floated, feeling weightless in the warm salt water. She hardly had to move a finger to stay afloat, and the bright afternoon sun warmed her exposed skin, already tanned from her daily outdoor activity.

It was glorious to spend an afternoon swimming after a full morning's work with Niko, and she looked forward to a leisurely evening when they would dine in the fragrant arbor under the grape leaves. Niko had begun teaching her Greek card games, as well as the popular *tavli*—backgammon.

Now, while the rest of the household napped, she could swim without inhibition, like a porpoise. After letting out all of her long pent-up physical energy by swimming out toward the rocks at the end of the point below the temple and back again, she had flopped onto her back, her spine arched, her ears under the surface. Then, out of sheer joy, she began to sing. Her performance consisted of American folk songs and a Greek lullaby Niko had taught her, one that Kiki used to sing to him when he was little.

At last, feeling somewhat waterlogged, she scrambled up the pebbly slope to the beach and ran toward the tree where she had left her towel.

To her surprise, the shadow of the tree seemed to move, and suddenly Kostas was there, standing face to face with her. He had a strange smile playing on his lips as he handed her the towel.

At first she was startled and embarrassed. All sorts of contradictory emotions raced through her. On the one hand, she was annoyed at his invasion of her privacy. Yet on the other, his unexpected appearance filled her with a girlish pleasure.

"Kostas!" She blushed furiously and practically snatched the towel from him to cover her bikini-clad body. "I didn't know you were back from Athens."

Although flustered by the glitter in his dark eyes as he watched her dry herself, she noticed that he was not in his usual slacks and silk shirt. He was dressed in cutoff jeans, the ragged white threads brilliant against his dark thighs, and a white Windbreaker that fell open to reveal a tanned, muscular chest. Except for that Mediterranean build, he might have passed for an American student.

"I came back rather earlier than expected. And as I heard your voice serenading me like a siren from the sea, I came from my balcony to see if you would go fishing with me. I understand the *psaria* are biting on the other side of the island."

Although this friendly overture was disconcerting and she was acutely embarrassed to think that he had heard her singing, curiosity got the better of her.

"Psaria?" she asked, rubbing at her wet, curly hair with a corner of the large towel and staring up at him in fascination.

"Fish, in English. Unfortunately, I cannot tell you what kind. They did not teach me the varieties of fish at the university."

Now she noticed that he had a canvas bag with him, and next to it something metal sparkled in the sand.

"If you have the energy, after your water ballet, to come along with me, you can sit on the beach and watch. I needn't worry about your becoming bored—you seem adept at amusing yourself."

Kostas was actually teasing her! She wondered if her less-than-perfect talents had brought that particular smile to his face. Then she remembered what Niko had said about his forthcoming marriage, and she realized the truth. Loukia was responsible for his high spirits. He looked years younger, his eyes sparkling at her, his perfect teeth revealed against olive skin.

"Yes," she answered, wondering with a certain uneasiness if he would now tell her of his engagement. "I would like to come, but not just to watch. If you have an extra line..."

"Not line fishing. I am going to skin-dive—what you call free diving—with a mask and snorkel. It requires a strong swimmer and can be quite dangerous for one who does not know his own limits."

"I've always wanted to skin-dive," she said impulsively.

His amused smile became condescending, and she saw again the expression he had had when he ordered her into the car.

"It will be too difficult for you," he said.

"I'm a strong swimmer," she persisted obstinately.

Kostas's male ego, she was beginning to realize, needed to believe she was really weak. Well, she would prove him wrong, just as she had on her walk to town, with great satisfaction.

With a skeptical raising of his brows, he gave in. "What can I do?" he said, shrugging his shoulders. "You have already made up your mind. There is an extra mask in the boat and some fins of Niko's."

He picked up his canvas bag and indicated the metal object that lay in the sand. "Your first duty is to carry the weight belt," he said in a commanding tone of voice.

Obediently, she leaned over to pick it up. It was twice as heavy as the weights Niko used for exercising, and what was more, it was not a solid piece, but made up of individual blocks of lead attached to a thick belt, so that it hung slack and threatened to pull her off balance. He was obviously taking his revenge for her stubbornness.

Out of the corner of her eye she could see a look of smug satisfaction on his face as he watched her. Well, she would not be the butt of his joke! She was athletic and proud of her strength.

Bracing herself, she lifted the belt from the sand as if the thing weighed no more than a towel, although she had to strain to achieve the casual effect. Then she swung it as gingerly as possible across her shoulder, trying not to grimace when it hit her collarbone with a thud.

She raised wide eyes to his. "Is this all?"

He laughed suddenly, and there was a glint of respect in his dark eyes. But he said nothing, only turned and gestured her to follow.

They went in his small motorboat past the point where the temple looked like pure ivory against the dark cypresses to a cove carved out of the cliffs on the other side of the island.

Kostas seemed sinister in his black rubber wet suit, but once they were in the water, Nancy became so completely engrossed in the undersea world she was encountering for the first time that she forgot to think about him. After a brief lesson in breathing through the snorkel, she got the hang of it.

This is easy, she thought. *I can do it without him.* She began to paddle away from him, but before she could go very far, Kostas swam up to her and grabbed her by the ankle, pulling her back toward him, his fingers cutting into her skin.

"You are an expert already?" he asked, his eyes immense behind the face mask. "You no longer need me? Despite your great strength, this is a dangerous sport. I order you to stay on the surface. Do you understand?"

A little frightened by his sudden intensity, she nodded.

"You would be less trouble if you stayed, like a woman should, on the shore," he said.

Before she could reply, he had taken a deep breath of air and disappeared beneath the surface.

The water was so clear she could see all the way to the bottom. The mask acted as a kind of magnifying glass, so that as she skimmed along the surface, Nancy could make out everything: her shadow on the bottom, elongated by fins; each ripple in the sand between the rocks; dark green seaweed waving with the gentle current. Most of all, she enjoyed the brightly colored fish darting around in schools and heading for the darker, deeper water when they sensed her presence.

Wearing the fins, she found she could travel quite far with little expenditure of energy, and as she was a good swimmer anyway, she had no fears of going far from shore. Kicking around a rocky point, she discovered shadows that suggested the presence of caves and watched in awe as a very large black fish glided out of the darkness, wiggling its tail with remarkable grace.

Suddenly an even larger dark shape slipped out from behind a boulder and followed it. After a frightening moment of pounding heartbeats and tensed muscles, she realized it was human and not some huge sea creature. It was Kostas, ten feet beneath her, and so intent on following the fish he seemed unaware of her presence.

How unbelievably beautiful he looked there in the greenish underwater light, his dark body insinuating itself gracefully between boulders, flattened at times like the current itself.

She followed him at a distance, so that he could not see her shadow, marveling at his patience in tracking the big fish. He only surfaced once for air during what seemed to her an unthinkable length of time. Then, at last, the fish started feeding in a seaweed bed not far from the beach. She saw Kostas surface, and moving his arms and legs very slowly so as not to scare his prey, he took a metal spear gun with a forklike harpoon from his weight belt.

Then he was diving again, sleek as a seal, and suddenly there was an explosion of bubbles. A cloud of blood rose where the fish had been harpooned.

Nancy felt a sudden surge of rage at him. How could he mar the harmonious underwater world with violent death? When they were both ashore and he had dropped the fish with the others on the sand, she was unable to contain her outrage.

"How could you be so cruel!" she accused. "Can't you get your aggressions out without shooting living things? Or is that your idea of being a sportsman, selfishly destroying for your own enjoyment?"

He stopped drying his glistening hair and looked at her intently, his fisherman's smile of triumph gone, replaced by a dangerous light in his eyes. His nostrils flared and his broad chest rose and fell rapidly.

"Is that what you think?" he said in the iciest of tones, as if he would have liked to throttle her. He towered above her threateningly. "You American women have an opinion on everything, whether you have all the information or not. Perhaps there are good reasons for the things you condemn."

Nancy wanted to back away from his tongue-lashing, but stubborn pride forced her to face him.

"Let me tell you something," he went on, "we all kill to eat, in America as well as in Greece. But the big difference between us is that you do not acknowledge that ugly fact, while in Greece we must live with it every day. You think that makes us cruel. I think it makes us honest. I hope you consider what I have said while you enjoy this fish at supper tonight!"

She glared back at him, but her anger and pride had given way to a feeling of shame. He was speaking the truth, she knew. It was one thing to condemn killing when one bought food in a supermarket. Yet, she thought, if the necessity for killing made the islanders more honest, then judging by Kostas, it also produced a kind of hardness in them, at least compared to the American men she had known. She could see that hardness in his father, too, but in Kostas it bordered on cruelty. Perhaps this was why he was capable of such indifference toward Niko's feelings.

As he peeled off his diving suit and stood on the beach in blue swimming trunks that revealed his muscular, well-proportioned body, she observed that all traces of his earlier friendliness were gone. A dark mood had descended on him, making him knot his jaw and glare in stony silence. He prepared for their departure with abrupt ungraceful gestures.

Her suit was already dry from the hot sun by the time he finished cleaning and wrapping the fish in plastic and stowing his gear in the canvas bag. Dressed in his cutoff jeans and the Windbreaker again, he waded out to the boat and pulled it in to the shore.

She handed him the bag and weight belt, which he tossed aboard, and then she waded out to the back of the boat.

As she pulled herself aboard, he took hold of her hand suddenly. "This is no island for foreigners," he said. "You will never understand our ways because you are not one of us. You cannot last."

He uttered the words with a harsh and strange passion, as though some special knowledge lay behind them. He was hurting her fingers, but she didn't dare to say anything.

Then all at once he let go and pulled himself over the side. He started the motor with an angry gesture, and giving her no time to brace herself, whipped the boat into motion. She had to hold on to the side to keep from falling over.

Nancy focused her attention on the water as the boat cut a path through the turquoise waves.

While she could admit that there was validity to Kostas's argument concerning the killing of the fish, she could not forgive his attitude toward her. She would have to show him she wasn't just a spoiled American, as he seemed to regard her.

The boat lurched again as they rounded a rock, and caught off guard, Nancy fell against Kostas. She pulled away from him immediately, but not before she had become aware of his sun-warmed skin and the smell of salt where the water had dried on his shoulder.

He turned to face her. "Do not worry," he said. "I will not spear you, too."

Before she had time to respond, his arm encircled her waist, pulling her close. Looking at his face, Nancy saw that the angry look had been replaced by one of amusement.

And then the amusement turned to something quite different as he bent his head down and pressed his lips to hers. His kiss was surprisingly tender, his mouth gentle and warm, and despite herself, Nancy felt her body responding. But the kiss lasted only a moment before he broke away. Chuckling softly to himself, Kostas steered the boat toward the Paradissis dock.

CHAPTER FIVE

WHAT DID IT MEAN, that unexpected kiss? Why, she wondered, should Kostas first caution her against any involvement with him, as he had done at the temple, only to embrace her—and after an angry confrontation! There seemed to be no answers to his unpredictable behavior.

Unless he had been playing with her. And she, like a little fool, had responded to imaginary tenderness when none had existed. That, she thought with a sinking heart, explained the supercilious smile. She felt humiliated at the memory of the passion he had stirred in her. But she would not, she thought adamantly as she dressed for her dinner at Barbara's the following evening, be made a fool of a second time. She might have been susceptible yesterday, but today she was wiser. She would never let such a thing happen between them again.

Then, as she slipped into a hand-embroidered blouse, she pondered his strange outburst. "You will never understand our ways because you are not one of us," he had said. "You cannot last."

The words mystified her. But why not? Did he believe that life on Korpas was so difficult that she could not cope with it, let alone understand it? Admittedly, there were things she had to learn, but there had never been anything she could not do if she put her mind to it. Surely Barbara was no more one of "them" than she, yet Barbara obviously was blissfully happy and well suited to her new way of life.

She had an opportunity to observe how well suited that evening, after she took a taxi to Barbara's house. Her friend's eyes held a special glow as she admitted Nancy to their modest apartment above the store. Panos, whom she introduced with obvious pride, was a man of medium height with hair of the light-brown color called blond by the customarily dark Greeks. Tortoiseshell glasses gave him a studious look, reminding Nancy of a young professor rather than a shopkeeper. In contrast to his vivacious wife, he was somewhat reserved, yet Nancy felt comfortable with him immediately, for his greeting was warm and he seemed genuinely pleased to meet his wife's new friend.

When the introductions were over, Nancy followed Panos and Barbara up a flight of stairs. To her surprise, they led to neither a living nor a dining room, but out onto the rooftop of the building, where a table was set with linen and china.

While Panos poured the wine, Nancy looked around her. They were not the only people out on their roofs tonight. Other townspeople were sitting on balconies and rooftops all around them enjoying the warm night air. The cafés and *tavernas* in the square beneath were busy, too, and bouzouki music wailed out of the open doors.

Panos handed each woman a glass. After a quick toast of *"Sighea"*—to your health—Barbara excused herself to go back to the kitchen, leaving Nancy and Panos alone.

Nancy moved toward the edge of the roof and leaned against the iron railing. At her feet lay the harbor, black and smooth as onyx, and at the end of the pier she could see a fishing boat just going out, a single orange light in its bow.

"Now I see why Greek roofs are flat," she said. "Even though you live above a shop on a busy street, you can still enjoy an outdoor life."

Panos joined her at the rail. "Tourists sometimes think they are impractical, these flat roofs," he answered, "especially the Germans and the Swiss, who are used to steep roofs as protection against the weight of snow."

"Of course a pitched roof would be impractical in a country with such a warm climate."

"Everyone thinks his way is best, and everyone finds another country's customs strange," he replied in his quiet voice. "Misunderstanding is the way of the world. These flat roofs have a very practical use. When Barbara and I married, there was only a small room above the shop, used for storing books. It was very simple for us to add another story, and now we have a large house, with enough room for a family someday."

"Everything looks so festive from up here," Nancy commented after a brief silence, "as if the whole town were having a party."

"What's this about a party?" Barbara asked, coming out with a large tray, which with Panos's help she set down on the table. From it she removed several covered dishes.

Nancy gestured toward the square below. "It's so lovely up here. How wonderful to be able to eat up here all the time."

"Yes, it would be, but the kitchen's on the lower level, so it's not at all handy for everyday use. But we do like to eat here when we have company. The view of the harbor makes up for the extra work, I feel."

Barbara's comment about the inconvenience set Nancy to thinking once again of Kostas's words, and as they sat down to their meal, she found herself wondering about the adjustments Barbara must have had to make.

"Tell me," she asked, helping herself to roast chicken, "was it difficult adjusting to life on Korpas after London? Were there many inconveniences to get used to?"

"Not when you're a romantic at heart!" Barbara laughed, passing dishes around to them. "But—" she paused to think, holding a plate of vegetables midway between herself and Nancy "—at first there were any number of things to get accustomed to. I was used to purchasing my food from the frozen-food section of the supermarket. I was the original fast-food fan! And I loved to spend practically all my salary on new clothes. As you can see, I do without fashionable clothing now, except for an occasional shopping trip to Athens. I hardly ever see any films or plays, but I find I read much more than I ever did in London. And I've even got used to cooking from scratch—the food tastes ever so much better."

Noticing the plate she still held in midair, she passed it on to Nancy.

"You're a fabulous cook!" Nancy exclaimed when she had taken a taste of the orange-flavored chicken.

Barbara and Panos exchanged a grin. "My wife was a terrible cook when we were first married," Panos explained while Barbara made a face, nodding her head to corroborate his words. "I began to think I had made the worst mistake of my life. But now, even my mother is satisfied with her cooking."

"Between my four sisters-in-law and a cookbook, I finally got it straight. The only trouble is that I have no oven. When I want to bake—as I did this roast chicken—I have to carry the food to the bakery down the street, where they do it for me. When you see women walking along the street with a tray of meat or cookies, Nancy, you'll know where they're going."

"Oven or no oven, this chicken is delicious. Will you give me the recipe, Barbara? When I go home, I'd like to make some for my sister."

"But you mustn't talk about going home!" Barbara responded quickly. "You've only just arrived."

"As soon as Niko's recovered I'll have to leave. And the way he's progressing, it shouldn't be all that much longer." She knew her voice sounded suddenly tremulous, and she tried to cover up her feelings by taking a second helping of chicken.

Panos turned to Nancy with a sympathetic look. "Perhaps, after all, you can remain here when Niko is well."

"I don't see how." She somberly regarded the heavy Samos wine glinting in her wineglass. "I'm afraid I can't afford to stay without working. And there's no hospital here for me to work in. Besides, my salary is needed at home."

Barbara looked sad. She wrinkled her forehead and shook her head slowly. "We'll miss you, Nancy," she said with feeling.

Nancy was surprised that these two relative strangers should be so sympathetic and caring after such a short acquaintance. Yet she, too, felt a strong attachment to them, which made her wonder. In New York, it had taken months and sometimes years of working with someone before a friendship developed. Here on Korpas things happened more quickly. Was it because she knew she had so little time, or was there some magic in Korpas itself that stripped people of their reserve and suspicion and brought out their warmth and trust instead?

"When I do go home," she said, "I'll miss the island very, very much."

"If you were to find a way to stay, I know you would never regret it," Barbara declared vehemently. "I have no doubt you'd be as happy as I am. I used to have spells of homesickness at first. Then last summer my dad was ill, and we had to go back to London. It was the first time I felt truly Greek—in London! Of course it was wonderful to see family and friends—but the noise! The crowds! It all seemed so frightfully unnatural, and I couldn't wait to get home. I discovered once and for all that my heart is really here."

She and Panos exchanged a tender glance as he took her hand in his.

Nancy couldn't shake the feeling of profound melancholy that had fallen over her. Barbara was telling her two things, she realized—the first, of course, was that she loved her husband. But the more significant fact was that Barbara loved the island almost as much, despite the lack of close friends. And the disturbing thing was that Nancy herself had fallen in love with Korpas without any realistic possibility of remaining.

"Of course, you have Panos," she murmured. "It's different for me."

"Then we must find someone for you," Barbara said with spirit, exchanging a look with her husband. "Beware—I am a matchmaker at heart."

"Please, Barbara," Panos interrupted laughing, "spare Nancy your attempts and let her enjoy her meal."

"Matchmaking won't do any good, Barbara," Nancy sighed. "There's no one for me here."

Barbara scrutinized her face intently. "Are you certain?"

A flush swept over Nancy's face. There was no question in Nancy's mind whom Barbara was referring to. The first time they had been together, her friend had made some pointed comment about Kostas. But if Barbara's self-proclaimed matchmaking skills were directed at him, she was certainly barking up the wrong tree.

"Honestly, Barbara," Nancy responded somewhat irritably, "Kostas is not at all like Panos. He's smug and unfeeling, and I find him completely unapproachable. I'm delighted to say we have very little to do with each other. And anyway, you know very well he's engaged."

"My, my, we are touchy!" Barbara was laughing again as she got up to put the dishes on the tray.

Nancy found it impossible to take offense at Barbara's good humor. She understood that Barbara would be glad to have a companion of her own age in Korpas—Panos's sisters were much older and all had families of their own. And what could be more natural than for her to imagine a match between Nancy and the most eligible single man on the island—or all of Greece, for that matter, considering Kostas's wealth and good looks.

But marrying Kostas! Nothing could be more preposterous. She couldn't help being surprised that Barbara imagined they were in any way suited to each other. Why, they couldn't be in the same room without flaring up at each other. And he seemed to be every bit as aggravated with her as she was with him, or so she had thought until yesterday.

"I suppose I am touchy on that subject," Nancy admitted ruefully, helping Barbara stack the dishes despite Panos's efforts to get her to sit down as a guest ought to. "But Barbara, I'm quite sure Kostas doesn't like me at all, although I don't know why. It seems as if he's been angry with me from the moment I arrived with Niko on the island."

"Or even before," Barbara put in, lifting the tray and moving toward the door.

"What do you mean?" Nancy looked at her friend sharply.

"I mean," Barbara answered, shooting a challenging glance at Panos, "that he made up his mind about you long before you left New York. He never wanted a person for Niko at all, especially a young American woman. No doubt if you'd been old, or Greek, he would have made the adjustment, but as it is..." She stopped and looked uncertainly at Panos.

"Barbara," he said to his wife in his gentle manner, "don't worry. You've said nothing you shouldn't have. If you would like, I will tell Nancy the story while you make coffee."

"Yes, please," Barbara said gratefully, and with relief on her face, she went through the door.

Panos leaned back in his chair, his forehead wrinkled in thoughtful concentration. One hand absently traced the embroidery of the tablecloth. When he began to speak, his voice took on an unfamiliar seriousness.

"I told Barbara to say nothing because I do not like to speak of this, but now I think you must hear the truth, for I do not like to have you misjudging Kostas. For if you think badly of my friend, you must think badly of me."

He paused to light a cigarette, then went on. "You see, I have known Kostas for many years—for all of my life. We attended school together here in the town, and later, for a time, at the university in Athens, before Kostas went to America. Since my marriage to Barbara, my friendship with Kostas has suffered. He has not been to my home even once, although I have asked him many times, and we have not been to his. Why is this? It is a long story. He had, one time in the California university, a girl he thought to marry. But when he brought her to his home here on Korpas, she disappointed him greatly. He discovered that she was—how do you say it—spoiled.''

Nancy regarded Panos's serious face in the half-light. She could hear sorrow in his voice and knew that he felt a deep affection for Kostas.

"Spoiled? In what way?"

"She quickly grew restless with the quiet life we have here. She did not want to remain on Korpas. 'If you love me, you must live in California,' she told him.''

"And he wouldn't agree?"

"Kostas loves his country too much to leave for a woman, no matter how he feels about her.''

"And so what happened?'' Nancy asked, finding herself increasingly curious about Kostas's past. Perhaps Panos could shed light on the behavior of this perplexing and complex man.

"She left Greece, and soon we heard she had married a very rich American. I think she was a fortune hunter, as you call it!''

"How sad for Kostas,'' Nancy said. "It's hard to imagine someone like Kostas being hurt.''

Panos shrugged slightly. "I do not think he really loved her. But his pride was wounded, and ever since then, he has believed that all foreign women are spoiled and could not be happy with the life here. He does not trust them.''

"That explains why he told me I could not last on Korpas,'' Nancy mused.

"Nonsense!'' Barbara had just come back through the door with a tray of fruit and steaming hot coffee. "How tough can life be in a house that has an oven! And a washing machine!''

She laughed and put the tray down, setting coffee and fruit before them.

"Now, Nancy," Panos went on, taking an apple from the bowl and picking up a small pearl-handled knife, "perhaps you can understand my friend a little better." He peeled the apple slowly in a single perfect spiral. "He feels things too deeply. He believes that Barbara will leave me just like the American left. And he cannot forgive me, for I did not listen when he told me not to marry a foreigner. We said some angry words. And so our friendship is not as it was."

For a moment his face was sad. Then he handed Nancy a slice of apple and one to Barbara. "But I am too smart," he teased, regaining his good humor. "I am certain Barbara will not leave, for I keep her locked in the shop all the day and at home all the night."

"Mind you," Barbara said, "I would certainly run off if he gave me the chance!"

She looked up at him and beamed. Her happiness was so evident that Nancy couldn't help smiling with her.

After the fruit and coffee, Panos went downstairs and returned with a bottle of Metaxa brandy, which he poured into liqueur glasses. It was the finest quality brandy, and Nancy felt the golden liquid diffusing warmth throughout her body. As silence fell over them, she once again became aware of the island around her—the fragrance of herbs from the hills, the whisper of the sea a stone's throw from the roof. She looked up and saw the stars above her, so close that she felt she could put her hand out and touch them.

In New York the stars were rarely visible at all, and even in Connecticut only the most brilliant were visible through the glare of city lights. Wasn't *this* the life people were meant to live—simple and close to nature? She wondered if Kostas, despite his wealth, felt as she did. Why else would he remain on the island when he could live anywhere in the world? Antonis, his father, had said as much when he had told her back in New York that the love of nature was "in the blood." And she had seen it in Kostas's eyes the night he had walked her to the temple.

Yet paradoxically he was so insensitive in other ways. Why, the very fact that he could kiss her with that glint of amusement in his eyes after practically calling her a spoiled child was proof of that. It was as if even the kiss was an expression of his condescension. Being with Kostas was as difficult and unpredictable as finding oneself alone in deep uncharted waters. She did not understand the pull of the currents, though she was aware of the danger of yielding to them. But why think of Kostas, she told herself sharply. Why not enjoy the warm air, the good feeling of friendship and superb brandy? With an effort, she brought herself back to the present.

While Barbara and Panos cleared the table and headed down to the kitchen—Panos winning out in his refusal to have any help from Nancy—she rose from her seat and wandered to the edge of the rooftop. The evening had grown quiet, for the shops were now closed and people had moved indoors. The air was fragrant with the scent of lemon blossoms. She heard the branches of the trees rustling with the breeze that had come up, and tiny waves slapped at the concrete wall of the harbor. Out in the black distance the lights of a cruise ship passed along the horizon.

The sound of guitar music caught her attention, and leaning over the railing, Nancy saw a group of people sitting near the harbor's edge, apparently the last patrons at an outdoor café. They were listening to a young man as he strummed the guitar, his rich tenor voice blending with the melodious instrument. As she gazed down at them, entranced by the haunting melody, a man sitting with his back to her suddenly turned in his chair and looked up. With a little gasp of surprise, Nancy recognized Kostas.

Instinctively she drew back into the shadows so he wouldn't spot her, knowing beyond any doubt that he was the last person she wanted to see this evening. Before she could analyze her curious reaction, Panos had returned.

It was late, and they were all tired—especially Barbara and Panos, Nancy realized, for they had been in their shop all day and had worked hard to make this evening's dinner party a success. And so she told Panos she was ready to go home.

She accompanied him downstairs and found Barbara in the kitchen, just finishing the dishes.

"Barbara, you should have let me help," she chided her friend.

"No guest in Panos's home is allowed to lift a finger," she answered good-naturedly. "If we ever come to the States, we will be *your* guests."

"I wish I could return the hospitality while I'm here," Nancy said wistfully. "Maybe Kiki wouldn't mind if I prepared a meal for you some evening."

Panos shook his head. "It is not possible," he answered flatly.

"Forgive me, Panos. I forgot. But how can I ever thank you for such a wonderful evening?"

"Your enjoyment is enough, is it not, Barbara?"

"More than enough."

Barbara walked to the door with them and, kissing Nancy affectionately, urged her to come again soon. And then Nancy and Panos were on their way down the last flight of stairs to the street.

Panos led her around to the harbor side, instead of to the street outside the shop as she had expected. Only as she approached them did she realize that the group of men and women she had seen from the roof were now close by, Kostas among them.

She wanted to turn around and go back into the house and let Panos bring the car around to the front of the shop for her. It didn't matter that Panos had explained Kostas's feelings to her. Too many heated exchanges had passed between them, and he had caused her to feel too many warring emotions for her to be comfortable in his presence. She didn't want another lovely evening ruined by his sarcasm or the venomous side of her own nature that she so disliked and that he alone could bring out in her. She wanted to go to bed that night with an easy mind, to close her eyes on a perfect day, with peace and warm friendship in her heart instead of anger and confusion.

But what could she say to Panos? He had revealed, against his wishes, personal facts about Kostas in order to make him appear better in her eyes. He would not understand her wish to avoid him. She had no choice but to walk on and hope that Kostas would let her pass without comment.

She felt herself breathing shallowly as she drew closer to the man sitting at the metal table with a tall thin glass of ouzo in his hand. He didn't sit like anyone else, she thought, and he didn't hold his glass like anyone else. There was in his attitude something aristocratic, an easy elegance that clearly made him the focal point of the group. She had no doubt that everyone present felt that difference and deferred to him.

When she and Panos approached the table, Kostas gave her a slow burning look. Then he turned his attention to Panos, rising and putting out his hand. The two men greeted each other cordially enough, not embracing in the Greek manner, but shaking hands and exchanging words in their language. Nancy stood by passively, waiting for Kostas to turn his unpredictable attention on her. She wished that Panos would take her away quickly.

Then she heard her name mentioned, first by Panos, then repeated by Kostas. The name sounded different on his lips than on Panos's. Kostas emphasized it in some way that made her faintly uncomfortable.

"But, Panos, I am going home myself," Kostas said suddenly, switching to English. "Nancy can come with me."

This time her heart lurched painfully. "Kostas," she protested, "Panos is taking me home."

He turned a withering glance on her, and she quailed.

"Will you have Panos drive all that way when I am going home anyway? That would be inconsiderate, would it not?"

What could she say? Of course she couldn't be that self-ish, no matter how she felt about being alone with him. With a show of self-assurance, she turned to Panos.

"I'll go with Kostas," she told him. "You go home to Barbara. And thank you again for a truly lovely evening."

Panos kissed her on both cheeks. "Nancy," he said warmly, "it was a pleasure for us to have you as our guest."

"Come," Kostas commanded.

She turned to look once more at Panos, who was receding into the shadows. She had hoped he would rescue her, but blissfully unaware of her feelings, he went on home to his wife. Reluctantly she turned back to Kostas.

After bidding his companions good-night, he guided her toward the Mercedes and held the door open for her. As he slid into the driver's side, he asked her about Barbara.

"You are fond of Panos's wife? She is a good person, in your opinion?"

Nancy didn't know if this was a safe subject with him or not, but she was glad of the chance to express her feelings about Barbara. Perhaps she could do something to bridge the gap between them.

"Barbara is a lovely person, Kostas," she answered, "and a wonderful wife for Panos."

"It would seem so," he said thoughtfully. "They have been married four years now."

"Yes," said Nancy. And then, unable to resist, although she knew he wouldn't understand her reference, added, "and she hasn't even got an oven."

"Panos cannot afford to buy an oven," he said seriously. "Who in this town can, besides my family?"

He started the car, and they rolled smoothly away from the harbor. "Panos must pay a 100-percent tax on such imported items as stoves or refrigerators or washing machines. His family has the money—they are not poor. But their land, which brought in the income, went to the four sisters for their dowries. So Panos must work hard to earn his money. Fortunately he owns the shop, so he does not have to live like many who have nothing."

The car was climbing the long hill now, beyond the town's lights. The sky with its brilliant display of stars seemed to hang even lower, brushing the hills with its light. Kostas continued, too wrapped up in the subject to turn any of his sarcasm on her.

"You see, there are problems with my country that must be changed in order for us to progress. One of them I will do everything in my power to solve: we must be able to manufacture our machines here. We *must* industrialize."

"And the other problem?" she asked, pleased to hear his opinions and at the same time eager to keep him on a safe neutral subject.

"Ignorance." He swiftly and skillfully negotiated the bumpy, winding road. "For instance, there is no longer any reason for a family to break up their income-producing land into parcels as dowries for their daughters. Yet it is an old-fashioned custom that continues today."

He paused comtemplatively before continuing. "Part of Greece's problem lies in its history. While the rest of Europe grew and became modern, my people were still subjected to Turkish rule, forbidden even to educate our children. We could not develop until we had thrown off the brutal yoke of tyranny, and by then we were so far behind that it sometimes seems to me we will never catch up."

He slowed the car and pulled up to the big white house. "No," he said, switching off the engine and turning to face her, his large eyes luminous in the dark, "if there is one thing I must do in my life, it is to help my people become modern. We must be a part of Europe, more of an industrialized society, even if it means we lose some of the beauty of our present way of life. As long as one person must live without electricity and running water, or is forced to till the land with a wooden plow, I will not rest in my efforts. Can you understand that?" he asked passionately.

"Yes," she answered quietly, almost hypnotized by his voice and moved by his ambition for his people, "I understand."

His intensity of feeling, his concern for the well-being of his less fortunate countrymen surprised and touched her. This was a new and quite different side of Kostas, one she had not imagined he possessed. Perhaps it was this side of him that inspired such loyalty in Niko and Panos. But could a feeling for one's people, fine and noble as that was, be any replacement for sensitivity to those closest to him?

She felt his gaze move from her eyes down to her mouth. His eyes lingered there, seeming to soften. She seemed to hear her own heartbeat in the quiet car. For once she was not afraid of what the next moment with him might bring. He had shared his feelings with her, instead of belittling or chastising her. She wished it could always be this way between them, for she felt better about him than she ever had before.

His eyes pulled away from her abruptly. He sighed and drew the keys from the ignition.

"When Panos told me he would marry Barbara," he said in an abrupt change of tone, "I thought it would be a mistake, although so far it appears all right. Still, only a woman born in Greece can really appreciate the life here and understand what it means to marry a Greek man. We are traditional people. This is why I must marry a Greek woman, so I can be sure of her. For she will be used to our life here. There will be no problems."

She listened with a heart that had suddenly grown heavy. She somehow had the impression that this had been on his mind throughout the journey, even while he had been speaking about his country, and she was certain that these words were aimed at her. The vague warning hints he had made were beginning to make sense. He wanted her to know that, as a man of tremendous power and influence, he would have to make the proper choice of a mate. And Loukia was that choice because she was Greek. Yet once again Nancy was puzzled, for she could not understand why it was necessary for him to tell her this.

"It has been a long day," he said, sounding suddenly very tired. A lock of hair fell down onto his forehead. "Tomorrow very early I must leave for Athens."

He got out of the car slowly and came around to her side to let her out. Together they walked up the dark path to the house. Kostas opened the door and followed her into the entrance hall.

In the grip of a sadness that had plagued her on and off all evening, Nancy wished him good-night. Despite his opening up, she was not quite ready to believe wholly in his good qualities.

Kostas took her hand in his, and his touch was gentle, "*Kali nikta*, Nancy," he said. "Sleep well."

The sound of her name whispered on his lips was strangely comforting. She seemed to hear it over and over in her mind, long after he had left her standing alone at her bedroom door and had gone up the marble stairs to his own room.

CHAPTER SIX

NANCY LAY IN BED for a few minutes after waking, trying to shake off the anxiety left by her dream. It seemed particularly strange to have had a disquieting dream about Kostas after their peaceful conversation the night before.

She searched her mind to try to reconstruct the details, and suddenly the dream came flooding back to her. She was swimming underwater, in that eerie, silent green world that entranced her so, when, without warning, her lungs began filling with water. Gasping for breath, she struggled to reach the surface, but couldn't seem to rise. Kostas's graceful form, clad in the black diving suit, appeared just ahead of her. She tried to swim to him, but each time she drew near, he darted away, looking angrily at her over his shoulder before he disappeared.

What did such a horrible dream mean? Was Kostas a friend, as he had begun to seem last night, or was he something else?

Dressing in shorts and a T-shirt, Nancy left the house and ran more slowly than usual down the path to the beach. Her body felt heavy and tired today, her mind fogbound. Perhaps the unaccustomed brandy and the wine at dinner the night before had left their mark. Breathing deeply in the already hot morning air, she jogged along the water's edge, unable to throw off her oppressive mood.

She began to reflect on the previous evening's events to try to make some sense out of them. Panos had attempted to explain Kostas's apparent disapproval of her. Yet Nancy was not satisfied with his explanation, for she felt sure that

Kostas was too intelligent to condemn all foreign women simply on the basis of a single bad experience. No, there had to be other reasons behind his strange attitude toward her.

Then there was that unexpected outburst at the end of their conversation, when Kostas had begun discussing Panos's and Barbara's marriage. Since Panos had already married his foreign wife, against Kostas's advice, and Kostas himself was already engaged to a Greek woman, why had he found it necessary to tell her in that urgent tone of voice of his own preferences?

Unless—the thought came suddenly and chilled her so that goose bumps rose on her arms and legs—unless Kostas thought *she* was another American opportunist. If that was what Kostas believed, it made perfect sense that he should warn her he was not to be had. But, she thought, stumbling a little in the soft sand, she surely hadn't given him that impression. With a sudden flush, Nancy thought of the way Kostas had kissed her on the boat and the undeniable physical response on her part. But then, she told herself defensively, he was very handsome and extraordinarily male. Surely he could not think that one incident meant she was interested in him in any romantic way when nothing could be further from the truth.

But such thinking was getting her nowhere, and she was rapidly becoming exhausted. The run had failed to restore her to her normally cheerful self. She would just have to weather the morning somehow and hope that the afternoon would bring something to take her out of the dumps.

As she walked back toward the house, she heard the sound of a car starting. Then the Mercedes with Kostas at the wheel rolled along the driveway and headed over the hill toward town. She remembered Kostas had said he would be going to Athens. He was probably on his way to catch the ferry.

How different the house seemed when Kostas was gone, she thought as she went in the front door and along the hall to her room. She wondered how long his absence would be this time. The last time Kostas and his father had been gone, she had felt that she and Kiki and Niko had rattled around in the big house like skeletons, and she had found herself looking forward to their return. Yet when Kostas was at home she was constantly on guard, unconsciously listening for his footsteps or the sound of his voice, bracing herself for an unpleasant confrontation or one of his equally unpleasant stony silences. She wondered at his ability to affect her well-being, whether he was at home or away.

Niko was on the veranda when she came out after her shower. Nancy smiled to herself at the sight of his cheerful little face, and her gloom began to lift somewhat. It was amazing what a difference every day brought in Niko. The sweet but pensive boy of the New York hospital had given way to an outgoing and irrepressible imp. Today she responded to the excitement on his face before she even knew what was making him so happy.

"Good morning, Niko," Nancy said, sitting down next to him at the breakfast table. "You look like the cat who swallowed a canary. What's going on?"

"I was thinking," he said, "that soon I will be able to run with you on the beach."

"True enough, my friend, but when that time comes my work will be done here."

His face fell for an instant, but then the smile sprang back to his lips. "We are not allowed to think sad thoughts," he informed her, "on my Name Day."

"Name Day?" Nancy poured herself a cup of coffee from the white ceramic pot Kiki had placed on the table and helped herself to a warm roll, spreading it with butter and orange marmalade. "What is that?"

"It is like a birthday," Niko explained. "In Greece, most children are named after saints. We celebrate the anniversary of a saint's day instead of the day of birth."

"And today is your Name Day?"

"Tomorrow. But I am beginning my celebration today because one day is never enough for me. Last year, before my accident, I had three parties—one in a restaurant in Athens with papa and Kostas. Another in our Athens apartment with my school friends. And the next day, when we returned here, Kostas took me to a little island where we fished and had our very own picnic and slept outside under the stars. It was wonderful, Nancy." He sighed at the memory. "Never will I have another such celebration."

"But of course you will. Each year will be different but no less wonderful. And how will you celebrate this year?"

"We will have a small party here at home," Niko answered. "Only papa and Kostas and you. And my two aunts, papa's sisters, who will come back with papa and Kostas tomorrow from Athens."

"Don't you have some friends your own age to invite?" Nancy asked.

Niko threw his head back to indicate the negative. "When I was small, I went to school here on Korpas, where I had many friends—the children of shopkeepers and fishermen. But when I reached the age for high school, papa sent me to school in Athens. That is where my friends are now, and they cannot come so far."

Nancy felt a pang for the boy, realizing how lonely he must have been feeling during the long months since his accident. He had not only been cut off from the normal activities of a young boy, but from his friends as well. No wonder he had grown so attached to her and relied so heavily on Kostas for company. Perhaps, she thought, it was his dependency that caused him to overlook Kostas's intolerant attitude toward his infirmities.

"Next year, Niko, you'll be back in school and can have your Name Day party in Athens again," she promised. "And it'll be the best one of all!"

"No," said Niko, suddenly looking older than his years. "No, Nancy. If you are not there, it cannot be the best one."

She leaned over to plant a kiss on his cheek. She did not want to tell him she was sure that he would quickly outgrow his need for her, once he went back to his school and friends.

"Now," she said, straightening, "let's get to work so you'll be in good shape for tomorrow's party."

She didn't know if it was customary to buy Name Day gifts, but in any event, she felt she wanted to present Niko with some special remembrance. And so, late in the afternoon while Niko did his lessons in his room, Nancy decided to go into town to shop for a gift. The trouble was, she thought as she reached the outskirts of town, she had no experience in shopping for young boys. She decided to stop at Barbara's shop and ask her advice.

Barbara was wrapping a package for a middle-aged woman, and Nancy, after returning her friendly wave, busied herself looking through the paperback books. By the time the woman had left, she had picked out two novels for herself.

"I intended to shop for Niko's Name Day," she laughed, handing Barbara the books, "and here I am buying for myself. I can't for the life of me decide what would be appropriate for him. Any suggestions?"

Barbara laughed, crinkling her small nose. "Rather like buying a fig for a king! I'm sure there isn't a thing Niko doesn't have."

"Don't think I haven't thought of that," Nancy said. "But there must be some little thing I could find before the party tomorrow night."

"Now let me think." Barbara came around the counter with her mouth pursed and her finger on her lips. "An eleven-year-old boy. That *is* a hard one. I only have sisters, you know. Why don't you ask Kostas? He'd certainly know what Niko would like."

"Kostas is in Athens."

"He'll be back, surely, for Niko's party."

"He'd better be," Nancy replied. "Niko's counting on it."

Barbara began to rummage behind a carton of boxed stationery. "How about a book? I've got some new westerns and mysteries."

Nancy shook her head. "Niko does like to read, but I'd like to give him something more exciting. He needs a lift."

"Well, then, how about a record? All children that age love music. And the Greeks on the whole are a music-loving people."

"That would be great," Nancy said. "Niko adores the American rock groups, but it would take weeks for my sister to send me an album. When he was in the hospital in New York, he nearly drove me mad playing rock music day and night." She laughed at the memory.

"Well," Barbara said, lowering her voice conspiratorially, "if you promise never to breathe a word to anyone, I'll make a confession. I, too, am an addict: *Voilá!*" With a flourish, she reached underneath a pile of comic books and magazines and produced three unopened record albums featuring top American rock groups.

"It will be hard to give them up," Barbara sighed with mock despair, "but for Niko I can make the sacrifice. I've just received these, but it'll be no problem to order more for myself."

"Barbara, they're perfect!"

Delighted, Nancy paid for the records while Barbara, after including an extra album from Panos and herself, wrapped them. As she handed the package to Nancy, Panos entered with a stack of foreign magazines that had come in on the afternoon ferry. He greeted Nancy in a friendly manner, before busying himself with his account books.

"Now that Panos is here," Barbara said to Nancy, "we can go have tea."

After Nancy added an English-language paper to her purchase, the two of them went across the square to the café.

"I am still English in one way," Barbara said, slipping into a chair at a corner table. "I need my afternoon tea!"

Dimitri took their orders and soon they were sipping tea and nibbling on small sweet pastries drenched in honey.

"What I really wanted to get you off alone for," Barbara said, stirring milk into her tea, "was to ask you about your ride home last night. What happened?"

Despite herself, Nancy found herself coloring. "What do you mean? What could happen? Kostas simply drove me home."

"That's all?" Barbara asked, disappointment plainly showing on her face. "When Panos told me how Kostas left his friends to escort you home, I was sure something terribly romantic was about to happen at last."

"Barbara, really! If you must know, we talked about the problems of turning Greece into an industrial nation."

"Oh dear." Barbara's face grew even gloomier. "This does sound rather hopeless. Did you try getting him onto some other more exciting subject?"

"Barbara," Nancy said firmly, "I know you have some sort of crazy idea that Kostas and I are about to fall insanely in love with each other, but you might as well forget it. Nothing could be more ridiculous. In fact, Kostas told me last night that he would never consider marrying anyone but a Greek. He was quite adamant on the point."

"Aha!" Barbara exclaimed, her face lighting up once again. "So the subject did come up!"

"You are totally impossible," Nancy laughed.

Barbara shrugged good-naturedly. "Did you never hear of someone protesting too much?"

As NANCY CLIMBED the path the next day after her morning run, she found the Mercedes back in the driveway. That meant Kostas and his father had returned on schedule for Niko's party, presumably bringing the aunts with them. But when she entered the house, the only voices she heard were those of Antonis and Niko, and from the harsh clipped way their words were spoken, Nancy knew they were arguing.

She felt a twinge of apprehension. It was so unlike either Niko or his father to be angry.

She tactfully slipped out of earshot and went to her room, where she showered and dressed for breakfast. By the time she came out on the veranda, Niko and his father were sitting at the table eating breakfast and behaving as though nothing unusual had happened. The aunts, she was told, would remain in town for the morning, visiting friends.

"Congratulations, Niko," Nancy said, bending down to give him a little hug.

"Thank you, Nancy," he responded. But when he looked up, Nancy saw the same hurt look he had worn in New York the day he found out Kostas would not be coming to visit.

Antonis chatted pleasantly with her about her stay on the island as if he had nothing but her comfort on his mind, but Nancy's thoughts kept returning to Niko. She wondered what had caused the look of pain in his eyes and what he had argued about with his father. But she could not ask him what the trouble was with the older man sitting at the table.

When Antonis had finished his breakfast and excused himself, Nancy had her chance.

"Want to tell me what's bothering you, Niko?"

He lowered his eyes and shook his head. "It is nothing, Nancy."

"Niko, I know you very well by now," she prompted gently. "I know just by looking at you that you're unhappy. Won't you tell me about it? Sometimes just talking can make things better."

"My father tells me I am being childish," he answered, not looking up, but stirring his spoon around in a cup of cocoa that had grown cold.

"Childish? About what?"

He lifted his head, and Nancy looked into eyes that had gone dark with self-doubt. Instinctively she felt a need to comfort and protect him against whoever had hurt him.

"Maybe father is right," he whispered. "Maybe it is childish to wish my brother to leave his business and be here for my Name Day celebration." His voice faltered.

Nancy took his hand. "Kostas won't be here? But I thought he came home with your father and your aunts."

"Kostas is still in Athens. Only papa came home."

Nancy felt her heart thud as the implication of Niko's words sank in.

"Niko, I'm sure that if Kostas remained in Athens, there was a good reason."

The look on the boy's face stopped her facile explanation. Never had she seen him with such a bitter expression.

"That is what papa tells me, and I know it is true. But I also know that my celebration is ruined. Kostas has ruined it."

Equally disappointed in Kostas, Nancy knew she must make every effort to hide her feelings from the boy and not give him more cause for hurt. And so, with great effort, she hid the anger that she felt rising up within her.

"Niko, I know how you must feel—betrayed and hurt, isn't that so?"

He nodded, great tears welling in his eyes. "It is true, Nancy. I feel like a small child, although papa has told me I must accept disappointment like a man."

"Oh, darling!" Nancy put her arms around him. "Remember, I told you it's not childish to feel things. It's not childish at all to be loving and caring. You have every reason to feel hurt. But also remember, Niko, that people often hurt us without meaning to. You must learn to understand that and to forgive."

But she did not fully believe her own words. It seemed unthinkable that Kostas could allow business to interfere with the infrequent pleasures of a partially crippled boy.

All the rest of the day, Nancy listened to the household sounds, expecting to hear Kostas's voice. She believed that he would, at the last moment, return in time for the celebration, and she could tell that Niko shared her hope, although he did not say another word to her about it. But the telephone did not ring, and there was no word from Athens.

As the afternoon darkened into evening and she knew that the normal hour for the ferry's arrival had come and gone, Nancy found herself feeling more and more resentful toward Kostas. She could not imagine what could be so urgent as to keep him in Athens on this of all days. After all, his father had made a special point of being here. Kostas easily could have returned to Korpas that night and left for the mainland again in the morning. As she remembered the canceled visit to New York and the sleepless night Niko had had to suffer, her lips hardened in a thin taut line. In the things that mattered, Kostas failed time and time again. Those rare moments of feeling that he had let her see amounted to nothing. Her initial judgment of him was correct: he was an arrogant and selfish man, utterly devoid of human kindness.

That evening she took extra care dressing to make herself as pretty as possible for Niko in hopes that somehow she could make up to him for Kostas's absence. She put on a pale-green dress with a full skirt and a low scooped bodice, which showed off her shoulders and neck. As she combed her short soft curls into place, she realized that she was trying to do for Niko what her sister Jan had long ago done for her. What lengths Jan had gone to in order to make all of her childhood occasions special—birthdays, Christmas, school events—so that the absence of their parents wouldn't deprive her of all of childhood's pleasures and the sense of truly belonging to a family. Nancy was filled with renewed gratitude to her sister and knew she was doing the right thing for Niko, even if it contradicted the Paradissises' ideas about the necessity of "being a man"! Thank God that she had not been left alone with a sibling like Kostas, she thought, for her childhood would have been grim indeed. No, Niko was going to get from her all the love and understanding he wasn't getting from his brother.

"Nancy, you look beautiful!" Niko exclaimed when she entered the drawing room, where Antonis was sitting with the two aunts. He stood up cautiously and came toward her with a slight limp, favoring his stronger right leg.

"Your Name Day is a very special occasion," she said solemnly, pleased to find him smiling once again.

"Come," he said, taking her hand and leading her to the antique sofas arranged facing one another at one end of the formal room. "You must meet my aunts."

The aunts, Thia Christina and Thia Irena, were as alike as two birds—both petite women with graying hair swept back into buns. Like most of the women Nancy had seen in town, they were dressed completely in black. But she saw at a glance that unlike the peasant women, they wore dresses that were well-cut and of expensive material, adorned with exquisite pieces of jewelry—small ruby earrings in Christina's ears and a sapphire-and-gold brooch on Irena's collar.

With bright eyes they turned to Nancy, clasping her hands warmly and nodding their heads as Antonis spoke to them in Greek.

"Papa is telling them that it is you who have made me well," Niko translated for her.

"I can't take the credit—Niko has done most of the work himself," Nancy replied, nevertheless feeling proud to have received praise from the exacting head of the family.

Antonis poured an amber liqueur from a crystal decanter and handed each of them a slim glass. Then they raised their glasses in a toast to Niko, wishing him *kronia polla*—many happy returns. The drinks finished, they went out to the arbor where Kiki had set the table with the best linen and china. As they seated themselves, Nancy heard her name mentioned and then Kostas's followed by rapid Greek. Niko giggled.

"What are they saying about me?" she whispered to the boy, who was seated next to her.

Niko had a mischievous glint in his eyes as he translated for her. "Thia Irena says you are very pretty and it is a pity that Kostas is not here to see you." He put a hand over his mouth to stifle another laugh.

"What else?" Nancy asked, consumed by curiosity and wishing her comprehension of the language had gone beyond the rudimentary stage.

"Thia Christina answers that it is just as well, because Kostas would lose his head."

"I doubt that," Nancy said wryly.

Niko seemed to have recovered his usual good spirits. To the unobservant eye, the disappointment of the morning was nowhere in evidence. But no matter how he joked and chatted, Nancy knew that Kostas's absence had cut deeply. And she was unable to shake off her own hostility toward Kostas for his thoughtlessness. He might at least have telephoned to offer his best wishes, she thought.

The meal was an elaborate one of many courses and included such delicacies as squid and an exquisite egg-and-lemon soup. After coffee and fruit were finished, Kiki came out carrying the gifts. Niko unwrapped a costly Japanese camera from his father, a pullover sweater and a handsome matching shirt from his aunts. Then he opened the package containing the records from Nancy.

"Where did you find them!" he cried. "Did you bring them from New York?"

"No, Barbara had them in her shop," she answered, gratified by his obvious pleasure and glad she hadn't bought him an article of clothing, practical as that would have been. The records were obviously something special.

Antonis leaned across the table toward her. "It seems you have made a wise choice," he said.

"You may not agree when you've heard them all day and night," she answered ruefully.

"I did not think Nancy would want to hear this music ever again," Niko told his father, laughing. "She did not seem so fond of it in the hospital."

"I'm not fond of it now, either. It's you I'm fond of," she replied and tousled his hair.

Before returning into the house with their brother, Niko's aunts shook Nancy's hand, wishing her good-night in Greek. When they had gone, Nancy and Niko remained outside for a time. Then the child yawned and finally excused himself to go to bed.

The night was glorious, the black sky lit by billions of brilliant stars. The Milky Way was clearly visible, looking like white dust thrown across the sky. She felt a vague restlessness, and as she didn't feel sleepy, she put her light sweater over her shoulders and walked down toward the dock, where Kostas's motorboat was moored.

How incomparably beautiful Greece was, she thought, with its ideal climate and simple way of life. The sea was rippled by a breeze from Africa, and the moon, as it rose, sent its reflection bouncing off the water, breaking into thousands of tiny dancing lights. The warm wind caused her breath to catch in her throat. She remembered her first night on the island, when Kostas had walked with her to the temple and they had stood in the moonlit ruins, struck silent by its stark majesty. One could be happy to stay here forever, she thought. Outside of this island, there could be little more to ask for from life. Except, perhaps, the love of a good man—something she had occasionally dreamed about, although she had found little time for romance. Her life had always been so filled with responsibility....

The silence of the night was suddenly shattered by the sound of a motor launch coming around the headland and heading straight toward the dock. Nancy remained motionless as the motor was reversed at the dock's edge, churning up the waters around her into white foam. A moment later a tall masculine figure leaped agilely onto shore. After a wave and an *"efharisto"* to the skipper of the boat, Kostas turned and came face to face with Nancy.

His eyes widened in surprise. Then, his face lit up in a smile. "A little late for jogging, is it not?" he asked. "Or have you come down to greet my arrival?"

She was unable to contain the pent-up resentment she had been feeling toward him for the way he had disappointed Niko. His obvious high spirits served only to gall her.

"You know perfectly well that no one had any idea you were coming," she said. "But better late than never, I suppose."

"Nancy." His voice caused her to stop her sudden angry outburst. "I am not accustomed to being spoken to in that way." His jaunty expression had vanished, and she saw on his face the cool look of superiority that frustrated her attempts to communicate with him.

"Kindly tell me directly what it is that disturbs you, instead of hurling innuendos at me as if I were too dense to understand."

What good would it have done to tell him what she thought? He seemed incapable of understanding the human need for kindness and consideration. To him such needs showed nothing more than weakness, a weakness that no "real man" ought to entertain.

"Forget it. It's nothing."

She turned and walked away from him, toward the path and the house. Her heart pounded savagely against her ribs as she felt, rather than heard, his presence close behind her. At the bottom of the path his hand grasped her arm. She tried to shake him off, but he gripped her hard, forcibly turning her around to face him.

"I said," he repeated in a low threatening voice, like the soft warning hiss of a jungle cat, "explain yourself."

Infuriated by his attitude, she threw all caution to the winds.

"I mean," she burst out, shaking off his hand and letting the anger blaze into her eyes, "that your little brother was counting on your presence at his party. Not that it matters to you, but up until the last minute he was waiting, hoping you would come. And you didn't even find time to telephone!''

"And?" he asked with an insolent smile, almost as though he found her burst of rage amusing. "What other complaints are you harboring against me?"

"I find it despicable that you have time for business but not for your own brother who, for some reason that I find hard to understand, adores you. Do you take pleasure in hurting him, or were you just too wrapped up in yourself to remember what day it was? I've seen you break that boy's heart twice, and it's obvious to me by now that you're nothing but a selfish—"

She got no further, for Kostas's hand again grasped her. "Let me go, you . . ."

His face showed no expression, but his eyes traveled slowly from her eyes to the edge of the low-cut dress. She felt the familiar warmth suffusing her body, drowning her anger in a wave of confused and unexpected emotion.

"I will not let you go before I have my say," he said. "Since you have seen fit to give me the benefit of your wise counsel, you will now have to listen to my response, Miss Nancy Spaulding. I believe in your country you would call it giving equal time."

She pulled and twisted, trying to get away from him, but he held her fast. "You come here from America," he went on, "and suddenly you are an expert on everything. You give me advice on my brother's health. But that is not enough. You must also countermand my orders, ignore my suggestions and criticize me at every turn. Yet you do not have the courage to give me the courtesy of hearing me out. Instead, you run away."

"All I know is that Niko is being hurt," she snapped back. "None of your excuses can make up for that fact."

"For your information," Kostas answered in the coldest possible tone, "it would have given me great pleasure to be here for Niko's celebration. And had the afternoon ferry not had engine trouble before it left Piraeus, I would have been here on time. As even you surely realize, some things are out of one's control. The ferry returned to dock, and it was necessary for me to hire a boat, which took time to arrange. Do you think I would have gone through all of this if I had not wished to be here?''

He let go of her arm. ''But had I not been able to be here as I originally had planned, then that is life—and life is not always fair, is it? Niko must not grow up expecting his every wish to be granted. There are disappointments in life, or haven't you learned that yet?'' His voice seemed to tremble with a new emotion.

Surprised at the change in his tone, Nancy looked up to see an expression close to pain on his handsome face. ''One must accept life as it is, not as we wish it to be,'' he added.

To her surprise, his words touched a response in her, and she recognized the truth in what he said. She had been trying to protect Niko from a reality that she herself had had to face—a reality that *must* be faced, if one were to mature into adulthood, she had to admit. With too much protection, she might have become unrealistic and incapable of surviving. It was true. Life did have its disappointments. Niko would have to accept that before he could be anything more than a child.

''But there was no word from you,'' she insisted, not ready to give him the satisfaction of knowing he might be right, ''and Niko waited all day. You could have phoned. You could have explained to him. As it was, you hurt him deeply.''

Kostas did not answer at first, but turned and began to walk away from her up the path toward the house. For a moment Nancy stood where he left her. She knew she was right about that one last point, for Kostas certainly could have telephoned. Yet she could see that Kostas had not been as callous as she supposed. He *had* tried to return.

She began following him slowly up the path to the veranda. At the door, Kostas stopped and turned to face her. As his glance flickered over her face, taking in the wide clear eyes and the independent set of her jaw, his expression hardened.

"You do not know Niko as well as you think," he said, looking away from her. "By tomorrow he will have forgotten all about this so-called heartbreak."

It was such an unemotional heartless statement that it struck her dumb. She had been waiting for some word from him indicating that he would make it up to Niko, but once again he was dismissing the boy's needs as if they had no validity. A person with an attitude like that was capable of justifying any cruelty.

She could have wept as she realized the immensity of the gap between her values and his. Could there be any communication while they occupied such opposite poles? Perhaps it was because she was, as he had said, incapable of understanding his ways. But at that moment, she was glad she would never have to know the ways and customs that made him think the way he did. Yes, she was a foreigner all right, and glad of it.

He turned and went in. She was left alone, shivering in the suddenly cool air.

CHAPTER SEVEN

IT WAS FUTILE trying to study, Nancy realized. Even though the house was still and the Greek exercise book Niko had given her lay open before her, she couldn't keep her mind from wandering back to the previous evening.

Her unexpected encounter with Kostas on the dock had left her shaken. Once again he had thrown her off balance. Just when she had been convinced he was a selfish and unfeeling man, she discovered he had done his best to return in time for Niko's celebration. Still, his dismissal of the legitimacy of the boy's feelings was unforgivable. She wondered why she couldn't simply accept Kostas for what he was, instead of becoming angered at his attitudes.

Nevertheless, she found herself unable to dismiss him as she would have liked. She couldn't deny that there were other occasions, brief moments when he had opened up to her, and on those occasions she felt a communion between them that overcame their differences. She had been aware of the bond that first night at the temple. Although they had just met, there had been a few seconds during which they had seemed to share some deep emotion. Perhaps it was the existence of that other, gentler, more profound side to him that caused her to become frustrated with his arrogant sarcasm.

She closed the book abruptly, aware of the ironic fact that she was preoccupied with thoughts of a man she had disliked even before meeting him. Looking at her watch, she saw that it would be another hour before naptime ended and she would have duties to distract her from her obsessive thoughts. What could she do with herself for that hour?

She got up, stretched and walked to the edge of the veranda, her eyes taking in the scrubby hills that rose behind the house. So far her walks had been confined to town, leaving unexplored the somewhat rugged terrain that constituted the bulk of the island. This would be a perfect opportunity to hike into the hills. She should have plenty of time to get back before Niko would need her for a card game or a swim.

Picking up the grammar book, she went to her room where she changed into sturdy blue jeans, walking shoes and a lightweight cotton blouse she had bought in the gift shop in town. This time she did not forget a sun hat, and she took along her camera so she could get some shots of the view.

She had seen the other side of the island from the boat on the day she had gone skin diving with Kostas. But the most spectacular view, Niko had told her, was to be found near the chapel, which was on the highest point of the island. Inaccessible by car, it could be reached by a number of footpaths, one of which began behind the Paradissis house.

The sun blazed overhead—not too hot for comfort, but warm enough. It was moving down from its zenith on its way toward the horizon and nightfall.

Turning her back on the sea, she started along the path, picking her way among small rocks and clumps of low, prickly bushes past the house. Behind the road to town the path turned and rose sharply toward the top of the ridge, where it and other low mountains joined to form the backbone of the island. The terrain got steeper and more difficult as she climbed. The loose weave of the blouse helped the perspiration evaporate, and the thick denim of the jeans protected her legs from the thorny thistles brushing against her. She pushed forward with determination, eager for whatever new sight lay just around the next bend.

She hummed to herself as she climbed through isolated, almost wild landscape, determined not to let herself think of Kostas and their angry exchange. At the low end of the ridge the path leveled somewhat, and she paused to catch her breath. The Paradissis house lay beneath her, a large white L, like a child's alphabet block dropped at the edge of the sea. Here the temple was almost indistinguishable from the reddish boulders of the promontory, and the whole end of the island seemed lost in the endless stretch of ocean, its waters as restful and blue as sapphire, fading off into a misty lavender at the horizon. There was no sound aside from the flutter of breeze from the sea.

Her heart sang with joy as she gazed down at the scene before her. What a magnificent view! What an island! Every aspect of her stay in Greece had filled her with happiness—except, she thought helplessly, one. Kostas.

Again, Nancy forced her thoughts away from him. Following the path once more, she noticed how the earth looked reddish yellow against the scrubby gray-green plant life. The path winded here along the top of the ridge, running over rises and down into hollows until it rose, some distance away, up to the highest point. There it finally dipped down out of sight, about three miles farther on.

It struck her as curious that such a deserted and relatively inaccessible path should be so well worn, but she was grateful for its smoothness. As she moved farther inland, the breeze disappeared, leaving the air hot and motionless. She was soon drenched with perspiration and her short hair clung in damp curls to her neck and stuck to the sides of her face. Nor was there any view here, for the ridge had flattened and become a sort of plateau. All she could see was an endless landscape of brush and rock that, while appearing flat, actually concealed dips and hollows. If it were not for the path, she thought, it would be easy to lose one's way here.

She had gone about two more miles and was beginning the long slow ascent to the top, when she heard a clanking sound, as if tin cans were being dragged along the ground. She continued a little apprehensively, and as she came up out of a dip in the road, she suddenly found herself in the midst of a flock of sheep. They were unattractive animals with small narrow heads and black faces. Unclean and badly cared for, they looked quite different from the fluffy sheep she had seen in the United States. Several goats bounded after them, the bells around their necks clanging and banging. A small yellow dog followed, nipping at the heels of the laggards.

The animals moved out of her way, parting around her like a stream temporarily diverted from its course. She understood now why the path was so well worn. Of course the island flocks had to graze somewhere.

Focusing her camera, Nancy proceeded to take several shots of them. Suddenly a man appeared on the path in front of her. Nancy gasped, instinctively stepping back. His features were twisted into a gargoylelike grimace, and as he approached with what seemed an almost menacing step, he scrutinized her from under heavily lidded eyes.

In such an isolated spot, to encounter a man like this! She suddenly thought what a fool she had been, coming here alone. Frightened, she backed hastily off the path to let him pass, wincing as thorns cut through her jeans.

The shepherd began to speak in a low and guttural voice, gesticulating excitedly as he talked.

Nancy shook her head, unable to make out a word. "I don't understand," she said in halting Greek. But the man only began again the rapid stream of unintelligible words, gesturing this time toward the top of the mountain and then to the sky. He finished and stood staring darkly at her.

When she failed to respond, he shrugged, touched his cap respectfully and walked past. Soon the clanking sound was inaudible, and her heart slowed to normal.

She wondered what it was he had been trying to say, but at least his respectful gesture assured her that he posed no threat. Besides, it was impossible for her to be frightened for long in such a setting. With a smile of amusement at her initial overreaction, she was soon making her way up the steep part of the final rise, feeling an ache in her legs and some shortness of breath. Beneath her she could make out the town just coming into view. At last she stood at the highest spot, directly above the harbor.

From here she could see that the town was set in something like a natural amphitheater, with the square and the harbor as the stage and the streets and houses climbing in tiers along a semicircular, gentle slope. Above the last row of houses the hills rose at a sharp angle, down which two gullies swooped from the peak on either side, fanning out and joining just above the last row of houses. These gullies were rivers in the rainy season, she realized, and the sloping streets of the town must become virtual waterfalls. It seemed not to be the ideal place to build a town, yet the rainy season lasted only a few weeks, she knew, and constructing the town where it was had made use of nature in another way, making it unnecessary to cut into the hills.

The town looked like photographs she had seen of sleepy Arab villages, with no sign of activity among the rows of boxlike low whitewashed houses. And from where she stood the square appeared to be empty, the fishing boats tied up at the pier looking like toy boats in a bathtub.

She took her camera from around her neck and snapped a few pictures, sensing that the photographs could not possibly capture the beauty of the original. And then as she advanced the film and slung the camera back over her head, she saw farther along the path the chapel Niko had mentioned.

It was getting late, almost four o'clock. But, she told herself, she could not return home without seeing the chapel. Fifteen minutes more, at the most, and then she'd go back and be on the veranda before anyone realized she had gone.

But the distances were deceptive. What seemed only a short walk took her another half hour. By the time she reached the spot, the sun stood halfway to the horizon.

She had seen several chapels like this on the mainland and on the various islands she had passed on the boat with Niko when she first came to Korpas. They often seemed to be built on a headland overlooking the sea, and Niko had told her that they were frequently named for the patron saint of mariners—Aghios Elias. Glancing somewhat nervously at her watch, Nancy hesitated before going in. Niko would be getting up now. He would look for her on the veranda, wanting to go for a swim. She hated to let him down. The hike had taken twice as long as she had anticipated, and she should be getting back so no one would worry. But curiosity pushed her on. After all, she might not get back here again.

In the whitewashed courtyard, a few geraniums grew in rusted cans, and an old, half-broken wagon wheel leaned against a wall. Inside the chapel, the air was refreshingly cool and slightly damp, the room rough and natural with homely religious ornaments on the yellowed walls. The floor was of unsmoothed concrete and was littered with cigarette butts, candle wax and matches. In one corner stood a brass device with half-burned votive candles in it. Fly-specked jars of olive oil lined the walls near the door.

She walked in and began to examine the altar. It was a plain wooden table, the legs varnished to an uneven inch below the altar cloth. The cloth was much-mended white linen and on it were two candlesticks that stood on either side of the table with an old leather-bound book between them. She opened the book and saw it was printed in the Greek alphabet, which she was just learning to read under Niko's persistent and patient tutelage. However, she saw no familiar words and realized that the Bible was undoubtedly written in a different Greek from the one she was learning. Niko had told her that the spoken language, called *demotiki,* was different even from that of newspapers and modern books, which were written in the *katherevoosa,* or pure language.

On each side of a curtained door behind the altar hung an ikon. The one on the left was of a female saint on horseback. The other was a male saint, perhaps Aghios Elias, a boat on the sea in the background. Beneath the ikons were odd tin emblems hung by safety pins and hair pins or propped up against the frame. These devices were stamped with pictures of body parts—hearts, arms, breasts, feet, hands. She made a mental note to ask Niko what they meant.

Her throat felt dry and parched, and she wished she had brought something to drink. But she would have to wait until she got back, for her watch now said a quarter to five.

On the other side of the chapel the hill fell away steeply to the sea. A steep path led down to where the water flowed onto a pebbly beach.

She gazed down, uncomfortably hot and sticky, her clothes clinging wetly to her body. She longed to have a cool dip in the ocean before beginning the long walk back. No one would see her here, and she imagined herself describing the afternoon to her sister, telling her how she had swum naked in the Aegean. After another look at the waves breaking on the shore, impulse took over. She was late as it was—Niko and she had already missed their afternoon swim and another few minutes wouldn't matter.

The path wasn't too bad, although she had to slide partway down. Soon she was in a shady cove, peering down through clear water to colorful pebbles and boulders and patches of whitish sand. She could see the shadows where seaweed grew and the dark spots where sea urchins attached themselves to the surface of rocks. The colors beneath the water were brilliant aqua and green, while the air was pastel, with a hint of pink and gold on the hills as the sun moved closer to its setting.

She intended to take a quick dip and then be on her way at once. Taking off her shoes and then her clothes, she laid them on a large rock and stepped naked into the water. The little waves were warm and tender as they lapped over her legs and then her waist. Soon she was floating, feeling freer than she had ever felt, wishing that convention would permit a person this experience more than once or twice in a lifetime. It was glorious to be in a state of complete harmony with nature. Her fatigue washed away with the water as she floated happily.

The sound of a distant motor startled her. It seemed to be coming closer, and the horrible thought struck her that it might be a fishing boat coming around the island on its afternoon run.

She made a rush for the shore, praying that it was a slow boat and would take a few minutes before making its appearance. Then she clambered out and ran toward her clothes. But as she reached the rock, her foot twisted beneath her and she fell heavily against the granite. A searing pain shot through the side of her face and her right shoulder and arm. Stunned, she struggled to her feet.

Somehow, despite the pain in her arm, she managed to pull the blue jeans over her wet skin, biting her lip to keep from crying. As she put on her blouse, barely managing to button it with her uninjured hand, she realized that she could not possibly return to the house unaided. Why, she would have had difficulty getting up to the chapel even with two good arms. If she could manage to make herself understood, she would ask for a ride back to town with the fisherman.

But as the motorboat turned into the cove, she recognized the angry-looking person at the wheel. It was Kostas who had come for her.

As he pulled the boat close to the shore and glanced at her with his scowling face, she felt his disapproval cut through her. His scornful eyes traveled from her wet hair, down along her blouse, which now clung revealingly to her damp body, to her bare and sandy feet.

"You will have to wade out to me," he snapped. "And be quick about it! I have wasted enough time looking for you."

Despite his abrupt and insulting tone, she suddenly felt terribly grateful for his presence. She was already beginning to have some of the symptoms of shock. She felt cold, and her legs were barely able to hold her up. She could never have made the five-mile hike.

Somewhat unsteadily, she picked up her shoes and socks and waded out to the boat. Kostas continued his tongue lashing as she climbed aboard, feeling faint with the pain when she put her weight on the injured arm.

"Did you not think we would be worried about you? To go off into the hills without telling someone is dangerous, stupid and inconsiderate! Do you not think we have better things to do than spend hours searching for you?"

"I am sorry, Kostas, truly I am. I didn't mean to cause you any trouble. The hills were so beautiful, and I wanted to see the view from the highest point."

"You seem only to think about yourself and what pleases you. If it were not for the old shepherd, Mihaeli, who told his wife that he saw the *Americanida* in the hills, we might not have found you at all. Fortunately, his wife works for the owner of the café in the square, and so it was not long before word reached me of where you were."

Nancy thought with embarrassment of her frightened re-action to the old shepherd who, after all, had only been trying to help, not harm her.

She came forward in the little boat to sit on the seat be-side him, and as she did so, he was able to see her at close range for the first time.

"You have injured yourself!" he cried, noticing the awkward way in which she used her arm. "Here, let me look."

She shook her head, feeling nauseated and dizzy. "It's nothing. I fell on the rocks."

"Let me see."

"No, it isn't necessary," she began, but he was carefully rolling up the sleeve of her blouse and examining her upper arm. A large ugly looking scrape ran from her shoulder al-most to her elbow.

Kostas's finger gently prodded the arm. "I don't think you have broken any bones," he said, his voice gentle. "But you must have taken quite a fall."

Sudden tears pricked her eyelids at the unexpected warmth in his voice. Then he took her face in his hands and looked closely at the bruises that were already turning pur-ple. "Your cheek is swelling," he said.

"I'll be all right."

Slowly Kostas took his hand from her face and started the motor. He backed the boat carefully out of the shallows and swung it around. In another minute they were flying across the water toward home.

Every muscle in her body ached. She hardly noticed the now bustling little town as they raced across the harbor. She thought at one point she would faint, the jolting of the speedboat hurt her shoulder so. But with great effort she kept herself alert. It seemed like a lifetime before Kostas tied the boat up to the Paradissis dock and she saw Niko limping down to meet them.

"Nancy, where have you been? We were so worried!" he cried. He was about to throw his arms around her when he saw her swollen and discolored face. "What happened? Are you hurt?"

"You can see she is hurt, Niko," Kostas broke in curtly before Nancy had a chance to answer for herself. As always, he was abrupt with the boy, but this time Nancy had no energy to intervene. Her head felt light and her legs threatened to buckle under her.

As Kostas's eyes scanned her face, her own eyes filled with helpless tears. Without a word, he seemed to understand that she had no more strength left, and suddenly he picked her up in his arms. Exhausted and with tears beginning to run down her cheeks despite her best efforts, she let herself be carried up the path and into the house. In his strong and reassuring arms she closed her eyes and let her head drop against his shoulder. She did not open her eyes again until he had set her gently on the bed.

He stooped over her, his face close to hers. She could not read his curious expression.

"You frightened us very much," he said in a half whisper. "You must take better care of yourself in future."

Wordlessly, gratefully, she nodded.

"Rest until Kiki comes with the antiseptic and ice. I will look in on you later, if you wouldn't mind."

At his gentle words, her body relaxed. Again she nodded. "I wish you would," she said.

He gave her a penetrating look, then went to the door. "I will tell Niko you are all right," he said. Then, with one more look at her pale face, he went out.

If it weren't for the throbbing pain in her arm and the knowledge that she was lying in sandy damp clothes on Kiki's beautifully made bed, she might have slept at once. As it was, she did close her eyes until she heard a soft movement beside her. Kiki bent over her with concern on her lined little face.

"Where are you hurt? Let Kiki make you better."

"It's nothing, Kiki," she murmured. "Only a few bruises. If it weren't for Kostas, I don't know if I'd ever have got home."

"Kostas was very worried when you were not in your room this afternoon." She rolled up the sleeve of Nancy's blouse and grimaced at the sight of the scrapes.

"Kostas go everywhere—to the temple, to the town. But no Nancy." She applied a piece of cotton to the top of a bottle of antiseptic and turned it over a few times. When she touched the medication to the wound, tears sprang to Nancy's eyes at the intense burning.

"Oh Kiki," she said when the little woman had finished with the antiseptic and was skillfully applying gauze and adhesive tape. "I had no idea when I left to take a walk that I'd cause so much trouble. Kostas was right to be angry with me."

Kiki bent over her confidentially, placing a cold cloth on her cheek. "When a mother is angry at her child, it is not really anger. Sometimes, when a man is angry with a woman, it is the same thing."

"Are you saying Kostas was angry with me out of concern?"

"Kostas very worried. Only once before have I seen him so very upset. That was when Niko had his accident."

"You must be wrong, Kiki. He was angry because he resented the trouble I made for him."

"Perhaps. But Kiki is many times right about such things." The little woman put a well-worn hand against

Nancy's forehead. "You sleep now, Nancy. Sleep and have sweet dreams." And she slipped out as quietly as she had come in.

Nancy sighed and closed her eyes, pulling the light cover over herself and sinking into the soft down of the pillows. Was Kiki right about what she had said? She was sure Kostas was upset because he had to use his valuable time searching the island for her. Could he have been genuinely worried about her instead?

There was a key here somewhere, a clue to his erratic treatment of Niko and herself. She wanted to think about it, to find the answer to the character of this man who was so deeply puzzling to her, but her mind lost its focus and she sank into deep sleep.

SHE MUST HAVE SLEPT through Kostas's looking in on her, and she would have slept all evening and through the night, if Kiki hadn't awakened her with a supper tray at eight o'clock. She managed to eat a little of the lamb chop and roasted potatoes, while Niko kept her company and tried to restore her to health through his own brand of medicine: laughter. She appreciated his attention, but knew that all she really needed was sleep. Yet she didn't have the heart to turn him out; he was so earnestly trying his best in this sudden reversal of roles.

At last Kiki came in to collect the tray, and when she left, virtually dragging Niko out with her, Nancy once again fell into a deep healthful sleep.

The first thing in the morning, she had an unexpected visitor. There was a tap at the door and Barbara Savalos stuck her head in.

"You are a lazy bones!" she exclaimed. "Why, it's after half-past seven, and you're not out of bed yet!"

"Barbara!" Nancy cried with delight, sitting up without regard to her sore body. "What are you doing here?"

"To tell you the truth, we were a little worried, Panos and I. Phillipa, the butcher's wife, told me you had fallen from a cliff and were seriously injured. I never trust her stories, but just in case there should be something to it, I telephoned Kostas last night. He told me what happened. Nancy, I am so glad you're all right.''

She stood back, regarding her friend. ''I must say you do look like you walked into the proverbial door. That's quite an impressive shiner.''

Nancy couldn't help laughing at Barbara's last statement. And it was amusing to be the subject of town gossip. She should have known everyone in such a small town would know everyone else's business. She herself, being a foreigner, undoubtedly would be a particularly interesting topic of conversation. How refreshing after the anonymity of the big city!

Nancy patted the bed for Barbara to sit down. ''It's wonderful to see you here. I wish you'd come every morning.''

''I visited here with Panos a few times before we were married,'' her friend said, sitting down beside her. ''That stopped, however, as soon as we became engaged.'' She looked around her. ''Such a lovely room. What a floor! I wish we could afford to have marble. One day we'll manage it, I suppose—marble isn't all that expensive here, you know. Of course there are more important things in life, I daresay, than marble floors. Wedding anniversaries, for example.''

''Wedding anniversaries? Barbara, you can change subjects faster than anyone I know. What wedding anniversary?''

''Mine and Panos's, of course!''

''Oh, of course.''

''And I have news for you, Miss Spaulding. You had better hurry up and heal because that black eye will hardly enhance your evening dress.''

''Evening dress? You must be planning quite a celebration.''

''Yes. We're having a party in a *taverna* outside of town. And I, for one, will dress in my finest, for I've not had a chance to dress up for ages. I don't know if Panos will recognize me out of this skirt and blouse.''

"When is your party?"

"The day after tomorrow. We don't plan our social engagements far in advance—there are so few of them. But listen, Nancy, I have more news for you." She leaned closer. "Guess who has said he'll come to our party?"

From the way Barbara was looking at her, her lively eyes sparkling with romantic mischief, Nancy knew at once. "Not Kostas!"

"Indeed, yes. You must be working miracles. What did you say to him about us that made him willing to come? When I spoke with him on the telephone last night about how you were, it occurred to me that I ought to invite him, although I was sure he'd never accept. But he was charming to me. He said he'd be delighted and were we really married so long and he was sorry he'd had so little time for social calls in the past. Then he told me you had said very nice things about me. I do hope he's finally gotten over all that silly business about foreign women. Panos has so missed the close friendship they had. Maybe this party will help heal the breach."

"I hope so, too, Barbara," Nancy said sincerely, getting out of bed and slipping on her robe, taking care not to hurt her bruised arm. "But he can be so unpredictable I wouldn't count on it. I never know what to expect from him. Just when I'm prepared to hate him, he does something friendly. And when I feel he's warming up and becoming human, he turns into an arrogant snob. He's the most enigmatic man I've ever known."

She went into the bathroom and splashed water on her face, grimacing at her image in the mirror. Barbara had not exaggerated.

"Please stay and have breakfast with me on the veranda," Nancy said when she returned to her friend. "It's such a lovely way to start the day, sipping coffee on the edge of the Aegean."

Barbara stood and smoothed down her skirt. "No, dear, thanks very much. I never eat before midday, and I've already had my coffee. Perhaps in view of the thaw, I'll have another chance to visit you.'' She went toward the door, then turned back to face Nancy. ''By the way, Kostas offered to drive us to the *taverna*.''

''Oh?'' Nancy wondered why Barbara had seen fit to emphasize this bit of information. ''That's nice of him.''

''Yes, it is rather. Maybe this time you can move on to more interesting topics than the industrial revolution.'' Barbara gave her a piercing look, then immediately broke into a grin. ''See you Thursday night, then. And take care of yourself.''

Nancy sat out on the veranda after Barbara had gone and for once let Kiki serve her breakfast rather than getting her own coffee and rolls. She felt fit enough to help herself, but Kiki seemed to enjoy babying her, and today Nancy was willing to let her do it.

As she spooned marmalade onto her toast, she heard the scrape of a chair above her, and a few moments later Kostas came out onto the veranda dressed in tan slacks and a patterned brown shirt. He moved a chair from against the wall of the house and pulled it over to the table.

''How are you feeling after yesterday's misadventure?'' he inquired.

She looked into his eyes, fully expecting to see mockery, but there was none. His eyes were flat and expressionless, as if he had just asked about a particular item on an export list.

''I'm still somewhat ashamed of myself, Kostas,'' she said, returning her coffee cup to its saucer. ''You were perfectly right about my being inconsiderate, and I'm terribly grateful to you for coming after me. I don't know what would have happened if I'd had to get back here all by myself.''

''I could hardly leave you to do that, of course. A shepherd does not rest until all his flock are in the fold.''

''Of course.'' She refilled her cup from the ceramic pot and took a sip of the hot brew. That was it, of course. The tenderness with which he had carried her to the house, that wonderfully comforting touch, meant nothing. He saw himself as a shepherd, and she was simply another creature to be accounted for.

"Your friend Barbara was here this morning, I believe?"

She nodded. "Yes, she came to see how I was. The town is apparently full of wild rumors about what happened to me."

"She tells me she and Panos are having a party for their anniversary. I have accepted an invitation to join them."

"Barbara told me," Nancy said. "She was pleased you accepted."

Suddenly there was a faint trace of the old sarcasm on his lips and a glint of amusement in the dark eyes. "And why is that, do you suppose?" he asked.

Nancy was taken aback. She could hardly remind Kostas of his avoidance of Barbara and Panos since their marriage. It wouldn't be proper to let him know she had discussed him with Panos.

"Barbara thinks you're very charming," she said quickly, hoping she had managed to cover up any awkwardness.

"Does she indeed?" Now the sarcasm was unmistakable, and he looked at her from under arched eyebrows. Nancy wondered how he had interpreted what she had said to make him take this tone. "And you? Do you agree with her about my charm?" he went on.

He seemed to be baiting her, and she had no idea how to respond. The truth was, she realized, she didn't know how she felt about him.

"I know you're capable of great charm," she answered carefully, her eyes dropping to the coffeepot in order to avoid meeting his challenging gaze. "But I also think you might learn to be kinder."

His hand, which had been resting on the table in a relaxed position, suddenly clenched shut. She trembled inwardly, expecting that the gesture was a prelude to anger.

"You set great store by kindness," he said. "I understand some of the most notorious tyrants in history were kindly men, good to their children and dogs. But tell me, Nancy, what else do you require of me? I should think I have been most kind. I have opened my home to you. I watch out for your comfort and safety. Why do you not think well of me?''

"You mustn't put it like that, Kostas. You surely know I'm not ungrateful for your hospitality. And I'm not asking for anything for myself. It's only that I honestly believe you'd be happier if you could be kind to the people around you, the ones who love you.''

"Who loves me?" He shot a look at her. "Ah, you mean Niko, of course. Yes, you have told me before that I am unkind to him. Yet, if I am as unkind as you think, do you not find it strange that Niko and I are so close?''

He toyed with the handle of a spoon for a moment, then looked up and said, ''But you are not being fully open with me, I think, Nancy. I wonder—is it only for my benefit that you would like me to be kind? Are you not, perhaps, thinking of yourself? If I were kinder, then I would not have chided you for your impulsiveness yesterday. Isn't that what you mean?''

His accusation hurt her. What had begun as a friendly conversation was quickly deteriorating into an all-too-familiar exchange. The warmth and gratitude Nancy felt for him began to vanish.

"I assure you I don't need lectures from you on my character,'' she said quickly. "I've managed to take responsibility for myself since I was a girl.''

Kostas leaned back in his chair. "So you tell me. Yet since you have been here, you have done nothing but defy me, even when I make suggestions for your safety. And you have continually run the risk of doing yourself harm. It is remarkable to me that you have not hurt someone else through your headstrong behavior.''

Nancy felt the blood drain out of her face. "You mean Niko? Do you actually believe I would endanger him?" She stood up, jostling the table so that the cup rattled in its saucer and some of her coffee spilled over. "I'll agree that I'm sometimes impulsive. I'm strong and I know I can endure a

lot. But I would never take risks with that sweet boy!
Never!"

His lips tightened. "You are making a scene like a spoiled
child. Sit down."

"No, Kostas," she answered coldly, struggling to main-
tain her composure. "I will not sit with a man who thinks
badly of me. Your insinuations have no basis whatsoever."

She turned toward the house, hoping that her exit was
dignified as she walked the length of the veranda and went
in through the French doors. She was trembling with hurt
and rage. Kostas not only distrusted her personally but
professionally as well. If she were free, she would leave at
once and return to the hospital where Dr. Davies and her
colleagues recognized her competence. But there was Niko,
her precious Niko, who never failed to delight her with his
intelligence and generosity of spirit. She could never let him
down, nor his father who had been so kind. Kostas's opinion mattered, but she couldn't let him drive her away. She
had a job to do, a responsibility to live up to. She would
simply have to avoid him in future.

But as she headed down the hall toward Niko's room, she
remembered the upcoming anniversary party. Kostas had
accepted the invitation and he was going to do the driving.
That meant she would have to be alone with him on the way
to town and again on the way back.

CHAPTER EIGHT

TWO DAYS PASSED quickly—two busy days with Niko in which she managed to avoid any more conversations with his older brother. The soreness in her arm had passed, leaving only a faint discoloration. When, on the second day, the sun began to set huge and golden above the horizon, Nancy reluctantly went to her room to dress for the party, dreading the inevitable moment when she would find herself alone with Kostas.

She had come to Korpas to work, not to socialize, so her wardrobe was limited pretty well to casual clothes. But Jan, always wiser than Nancy about such things, had insisted she buy one dress for evenings out. It was an expensive but simple ankle-length sleeveless dress of fawn-colored jersey. Fancy clothes had never suited her, but the simplicity of this dress appealed to her.

The only jewelry she wore was a delicate gold chain around her neck, and a little makeup concealed what remained of her bruises. Reasonably satisfied with her appearance, she closed the door behind her. As she reached the front door, Kostas came down the stairs.

She had never before seen him dressed in anything but casual clothes. Tonight he wore a suit, cut in a fashionable continental style that gave him an elegant man-of-the-world look. When he approached her along the green marble floor, she caught a trace of the expensive after-shave she had smelled that day in his room, the day she had discovered the photograph of Loukia on his desk.

Kostas's eyes swept over her body as if he could see through the clinging fabric to her bare skin. "You look different in a dress," he said, his eyes crinkling with good humor. He touched her bare arm with his hand. "In fact, you look quite bewitching. I know few women who would dare to appear in such a simple garment."

Nancy smiled, absurdly pleased at his obvious admiration. He held the front door open for her and gallantly escorted her to his waiting car.

"Indeed, this is as it should be—a woman ought to adorn a dress, rather than the other way around."

While he walked around to his side of the Mercedes, she tried to adjust to this new turn in their relationship. Apparently they were not to argue tonight, but were supposed to be charming and civilized with each other. Very well, she thought, if he wanted to call a truce, she would be glad to do the same. In fact, it would be quite a relief. She would ask him about his business and head him away from any subject that might provoke sparks.

By tacit agreement, the strategy worked. In response to her inquiries, he spoke about the beginnings of the Paradissis company all the way to town. And although her questions were initially only a diversionary tactic, Nancy found herself caught up in the story of how his father had started the import business in Athens. There was no doubt in her mind, as she listened to him tell of the shrewd business moves that had eventually built a small empire, that when and if Kostas ever got around to telling her his role in building the company, she would find it equally fascinating.

After they picked up Barbara and Panos, Barbara took over the conversation. She was positively sparkling, both in disposition and attire, dressed in a black knit dress with gold threads running through it. She and Panos sat in the plush back seat of the car, holding hands and looking as happy with each other as if they had just fallen in love.

All of them were in good spirits as they rode out of town in the opposite direction from the Paradissis house and up into the dark hills. Soon they arrived at a brightly lit *taverna* with several cars parked around it and the sound of bouzouki music coming from within.

It was a small restaurant in the country style, which meant the whitewashed walls were unadorned. But for this occasion, the owner had strung up red and white crepe paper and put paper lanterns over the light bulbs. Brightly colored tablecloths added to the party feeling.

Nancy was introduced to Panos's mother and his four sisters, their husbands and children, along with a half dozen aunts, uncles and cousins. There were about thirty people sitting at the tables, which had been placed in a sort of T-shape, with Barbara and Panos at the head. There was much noise and laughter, kissing and hugging, until finally the wife of the *taverna* owner brought in wine. Then, when the glasses were filled, the men rose in turn to toast the couple.

Every word was in Greek. Nancy, who had been sitting beside one of the cousins, was bewildered until suddenly she felt a stir at her side. When she looked, she found that the young man was on his way to another chair and Kostas was at her elbow.

"Panos's father," he whispered, indicating the small wiry man standing with a glass in his hand. "He has just finished telling Panos that a good marriage is like a good wine—sweet to the taste, heady to the senses and better with time. Would you say he is right?"

"I know even less about marriage than about wine," she whispered back, feeling oddly self-conscious.

"I find that hard to believe," he responded, his eyes glittering. "Unless the men in New York are blind. Surely you have had many opportunities to marry. How is it that you have remained single?"

"My professional training and my career have taken all my time."

He looked at her skeptically. "To the exclusion of love?"

He was relating to her on a personal level, and she found it unnerving. Although she had wished for him to display an interest in her feelings and her background, now that he was doing so she found herself wanting him to change the subject.

"In America we wait for the right one to come along," she answered, a blush staining her cheeks.

He eyed her for a few seconds, then said, "Sometimes it is difficult to know who is the right one." His face hardened. "That is why an arranged match often succeeds where romantic marriages fail—despite Panos's obvious good luck. But I believe it is my turn to say a few words."

He rose, glass in hand, and Nancy felt a slight apprehension. After what he had just said, and knowing how he had felt these past five years about Panos's marriage to Barbara, she wondered what he would find to say. But as she looked at him towering above everyone, so handsome and self-assured, Nancy felt her senses quicken. He had too much natural diplomacy to embarrass Panos in public. In front of others he had never been anything but flawlessly polite, even to her.

In an extraordinary gesture of courtesy to Barbara, Kostas gave the toast first in English.

"I drink to your anniversary, Barbara and Panos," he said in a quiet tone that nevertheless carried easily to every ear.

"Wise men say that to strive against odds and to overcome them is the only route to true happiness. You have surmounted the difficulties of coming together from different customs and ideas. The reward—happiness—is evident to all of us tonight. Your joy brings great joy to all your friends. *Sigharitiria!* Congratulations!"

Panos's eyes shone with emotion as he looked at his boyhood friend. Barbara's face had grown serious, and Nancy could see Kostas's words had meant a lot to her. There was no doubt in her mind that Kostas had been utterly sincere.

As Kostas translated his words into Greek and everyone cheered, Nancy knew she had witnessed a special moment.

At last the meal was served. First came an appetizer of artichoke hearts in yogurt sauce, followed by deep-fried eggplant. A savory roast lamb was served next, accompanied by salad and crisp, oven-roasted potatoes.

At last, satisfied and slightly tipsy from the wine, the diners pushed back their chairs to clear a space for dancing. Two of the men went into another room and came out with musical instruments.

It was the men who got up to dance to the bouzouki and fiddle music. Among them was Panos, who stood with his arms linked across the shoulders of Kostas on the one side and his father on the other. They danced in perfect unison, and Nancy noticed how restrained the music and movements were, the dancers looking as if they were holding back, promising some wild burst that never came. And she also noticed how a man's body was suited to the steps of the *sirtaki* dance far more than a woman's, for the hips and shoulders were held absolutely rigid while all the action was in the leg. When she danced, she knew, she moved her hips and shoulders, as a woman is inclined to do.

In spite of herself, her attention focused on Kostas. She observed that he danced with more dignity and grace than the other men. Too, she had never seen his face so relaxed and happy. His large dark eyes were gleaming, the well-shaped lips were formed in a smile. His head was thrown back in enjoyment.

Suddenly he caught her looking at him. Something like electricity sparked between them. For a long moment their gazes were locked, and she felt powerless to look away. Everything else in the room seemed to have stopped. She couldn't hear the music or see the dancers or even feel the wineglass in her hand. But suddenly the music ended and the spell was broken. There was a burst of good-natured heckling, and then the dancers returned to their seats.

Nancy waited with nervous anticipation for Kostas to return, but he went right over to Panos's empty chair and sat next to Barbara. He put his hand on her arm, and although Nancy could not hear their words, she could tell they were talking like two old friends.

"You see what a good man my friend Kostas is," came Panos's voice close to her ear. She turned and invited him to sit down.

"What a lovely party this is, Panos," she said with feeling. "Your family is so friendly. And yes, Kostas certainly has shown how much he cares for you." She felt a glow as she said this and didn't stop to wonder why.

"I believe it is your doing, Nancy. Without you, he would never have come tonight. Barbara and I owe you a debt."

"I don't know what I had to do with it."

"I do not understand, either. But I am certain it is so."

"Well, Panos, the reason doesn't matter. Let's just be glad you've become friends again."

At last the long evening was over and the party began to break up. Tired, but still in high spirits, the guests went out to their cars.

"Oh, no!" Barbara exclaimed at the door. "It's raining."

Rain was coming down in sheets. Putting their wraps over their heads, they made a dash for the car.

"Never," muttered Kostas as he hurriedly threw open the car door for Barbara and Nancy, "have we had rain at this time of year."

"You are wrong there, my friend," Panos said. "Five years ago it rained for one whole day and a night. A very strong rain, like winter."

The men got in, and Kostas started the engine. "How can you be sure, Panos? I do not remember such a rain."

Panos and Barbara both started to laugh. "I'll tell you, Kostas," giggled Barbara from the back seat. "It was the day we came back from our honeymoon in Rome. All the windows were open in our bedroom because Panos's sister,

Elektra, had aired the room. When we came back the bed was soaked through."

"We were forced to spend the night in the hotel, like tourists," Panos said with a laugh.

The rain softened to a steady drizzle and soon stopped altogether as Kostas drove slowly along the slick curving road. As they came up over one particular rise, the sea lay beneath them. A full moon shone above the dark clouds, lighting a path across the water toward them.

"Oh," breathed Barbara, "how beautiful! Do stop, Kostas."

"Please do," Nancy seconded.

Kostas pulled the car off to the side of the road. He opened his door and stepped out, then suddenly shouted something in Greek. From the tone of his voice, Nancy knew the utterance was not for mixed company.

He leaned back into the car. "Mud," he announced. "We are in mud. It must have been raining for hours, all during the party."

"Oh, no!" wailed Barbara. "Does that mean we're stuck?"

"I would say so, since I have just stepped in mud up to my ankles." He looked seriously at each of them in turn, and Nancy felt a sudden urge to laugh at his expression. There was something so incongruous about the image of the elegantly clad Kostas standing ankle deep in mud.

"I am sorry to say this to you," he went on, "but if I am to get the car free again, you will all have to get out."

"Kostas, is there no other way?" asked Panos. "Barbara's silk shoes! Her new dress!"

"Don't worry about me, my love," his wife answered quickly. "I can take the shoes off. As for the dress, your sisters will tell me how to clean it. They can do anything."

"We'll all take our shoes off and join you in the mud, Kostas," Nancy said, barely able to stifle her giggles.

He gave her a keen glance. "And you find this funny—to be stuck in the mud on the edge of a cliff?"

At his vexed expression, Nancy could not control herself and she began to laugh.

"I'm sorry," she gasped, trying to assume a sober expression. "I know it isn't funny, really, but I just can't help it. It's so ridiculous, the four of us in our best clothes, stuck in the mud."

Barbara joined her laughter. "And to think I made a special trip to Athens to find this dress!"

Panos and Kostas exchanged an amused glance as if to say "women!"

Nancy slipped off her shoes and swung open the car door. "We can help push, Kostas," she said cheerfully, although she had just felt her toes slip down into the soft ooze and knew her hem must be brushing the mud.

"But your arm," Kostas reminded her. "You will hurt yourself."

"Don't worry, it's fine."

With a wary look, he assented and turned to Panos. "Will you drive, Panos?" Kostas asked. "You weigh less than I do. I can push while you try to work the car out."

Barbara and Kostas and Nancy stood behind the vehicle while Panos tried to free it, but the rear wheels kept working deeper and deeper into the mud. The more they pushed, the sillier they felt, and Nancy and Barbara kept collapsing against the car in fits of laughter.

"Do you think we ought to consider walking home?" Barbara asked at last, her dress completely wet down the front from leaning against the car.

"It is a long way," Kostas reminded her, "and you are in high heels."

"Then whatever shall we do?"

Nancy had an idea. "Kostas," she suggested tentatively, "I'm sure I saw a stone wall around that last bend. Do you think there might be some flat stones we could use to put under the rear wheels?"

"You have a good head," Kostas said, and there was admiration in his eyes as he looked at her. "That is what we must do."

"I will go," Panos offered. But feeling that since she was wet anyway and he was dry, Nancy decided that she would go with Kostas to carry back the stones.

The moon shed its light through a gentle drizzle as Nancy and Kostas walked back up the road toward the wall she had seen. They said nothing at first, but after Kostas had selected two particularly flat stones and had lifted one into her arms, he asked her again if she was sure her arm could take it.

When she again told him not to worry, he said, "You have much fortitude, Nancy. Many women would not have left the safety of the car."

His praise warmed her chilled body. "But we were all in the same predicament, Kostas," she protested. "And really, it's turned into quite an adventure."

"Your dress is ruined." She saw his eyes move over her body where the wet dress clung even more closely than before to her willowy figure. "It will never come clean, I think."

"It's only a dress. You aren't worried about your suit, are you?"

"I do not worry about my clothes when there are people to take care of."

"Nor do I."

He smiled at her in the moonlight. His eyes held a warm look of friendship and a kind of happiness she had never seen there before. Was she wrong, or was there a kind of bond between them brought on by the emergency? She remembered hearing how a blackout had once caused everyone in the New York subway to become friendly and cooperative. Total strangers had begun telling each other their life stories, and people who hadn't spoken to another human being for days were comforting frightened women and children. She was glad that the car had got stuck in the mud so she could know this moment of intimacy with Kostas.

When Barbara saw the two of them struggling with their stones through the increasing downpour, she once again began to laugh.

"Drowned rats," she said. "For good-looking people, I must say you two look absolutely awful. If only I had my camera."

"Look at yourself," said Kostas, joining in her laughter. "I hope your husband's sister can work miracles. Only Panos is dry."

At last they got the car out. Tired and muddy and absolutely exhausted, they drove back to town. As Kostas dropped Panos and Barbara off at their house, Barbara said, "Kostas, I will never forget this anniversary as long as I live."

"Nor will I," added Panos, and it was obvious he meant something different from Barbara as he embraced his boyhood friend. "You will come to supper some time?"

"Yes, Panos. Certainly I will."

Nancy let her head drop against the headrest and closed her eyes. The patter of rain on the car roof was hypnotic, and she felt herself almost dozing off when Kostas pulled up beside the house. He turned off the engine.

"Nancy, we have arrived," he said softly. "Are you awake?"

Nancy opened her eyes to see him watching her in the darkness. Her breath caught at the sight of his strong face etched in moonlight and the dark expanse of his powerful shoulders. She sat up, feeling wistful at the thought of ending the evening.

"You enjoyed yourself tonight, I think," he said.

"Yes, very much."

"I could see it in your face. You even enjoyed the mud."

Nancy laughed, and the sadness dissolved. "Yes, you're right. Even the mud."

"For that I apologize."

"But it was wonderful fun, Kostas. And I am so happy you and Panos and Barbara are friends again." Nancy decided not to worry about the fact that her statement gave away that she had discussed Kostas with Barbara and Panos.

Kostas eyed her sharply. "I, too."

He leaned close, so close that Nancy could smell the cologne mingling with his own musky scent. She saw the long silky fringe of his eyelashes, the faint cleft in his chin. She remembered the night they had gone to the temple and he had suddenly approached her. She had been alarmed then, but now, she found herself recalling how it had felt to be embraced by him, his sensual mouth on her own. The memory left her weak, and she realized that that was what she wanted him to do. To kiss her again, as he had on the boat the day they had gone skin diving.

"I think perhaps you and I might also be friends," he said, and instead of taking her in his arms, he extended his hand. In place of relief at the friendly gesture, Nancy felt a keen disappointment sweep over her.

"Yes, Kostas," she said softly. "I think we might."

Suddenly he threw back his head and laughed—a deep rich sound that filled the car. "By God, I will always remember this night," he exclaimed, opening the car door. "And not only because of the mud."

THE NEXT DAY the weather was once again sunny and clear. Nancy slept later than usual, awakening refreshed and filled with energy. It seemed that after last night she and Kostas were going to be friends at last. The breach that had been healed between Kostas and the Savaloses had extended to her. And now that he accepted Barbara, he could also view her without suspicion. The difficult time with him was over, and she could look forward to enjoying the rest of her stay on Korpas free from the hostilities that had marred their relationship from the very first.

She quickly dressed and headed down to the beach, her spirits as light and free as her lithe body.

As she ran along the hard sand at the water's edge, she was surprised to see a luxurious gleaming white yacht moored next to Kostas's motorboat. There were no other houses nearby, and as Antonis Paradissis had returned to Athens for an extended stay, she reasoned that the owner of the vessel must be a friend of Kostas's. At once she remembered the photograph she had seen on Kostas's desk. The visitor, she was sure, was Loukia.

As she climbed the pebbly path from the beach to the house, the sound of lively laughter and voices seemed to tumble down the hillside toward her. At the top of the path, Nancy paused. Kostas, Niko and a group of four men and two women were sitting on the veranda around the large umbrella-topped table. Kiki, her small body a bundle of energy, was busily setting cups and saucers on the table.

Not knowing if she would be intruding, Nancy stood uncertainly. She wondered whether to join the group or if it would be better to slip around to the back of the house and take her breakfast in the kitchen. As she deliberated, she saw the young woman who was sitting closest to Kostas lean over, and in an intimate gesture, brush his cheek with her hand. He reached out and took her hand in his for a brief moment.

Nancy turned abruptly away with a curious sinking sensation and was about to go around to the kitchen when Niko spotted her and called her name. The group at the table fell silent and turned toward her with curiosity. She had no choice but to join them.

Even with the over-sized sunglasses, which seemed to cover half her face, Loukia was beautiful, Nancy noted. The photograph had not done her justice. Slim and olive-skinned, her sleek jet hair swept off her oval face by a large silver barrette, she was simply clad in crisp white pants and a white silk blouse open at the throat. The other young people were equally smartly dressed, but Loukia shone from among them like a fiery diamond. Every small detail of her appearance bespoke elegance and wealth.

"This is Miss Nancy Spaulding," Kostas said, rising to make the necessary introductions, "Niko's physical therapist."

Loukia gracefully inclined her head and smiled at Nancy. "I am so happy to meet you, Nancy," she said charmingly, with a flash of white teeth. "You must be very good to have our little Niko looking so well. Why, it almost seems as though nothing had happened to him at all." She directed her lovely smile to Niko. "Aren't you grateful, Niko, dear?"

Instead of returning her smile, Niko dropped his eyes to his plate and said nothing, only nodding rather sullenly.

"I was surprised," she continued in her melodious voice, showing no sign of having noticed Niko's lack of response, "when Kostas told me it was necessary for the boy to have someone. I thought when he left the hospital he would be finished with doctors and nurses."

"Yes it's true, he doesn't need doctors and nurses anymore, Miss Kassandras," Nancy explained. "My job is to follow up the doctor's work until Niko regains the full use of his limbs."

"I, for one, am delighted Nancy is here," said a ruddy-faced Englishman introduced to her as Martin. "She gives us an excuse to switch to English, thank heavens!" He gallantly moved his chair to make room for her. "Will you be joining us for breakfast, Nancy?"

Feeling self-conscious in her shorts and T-shirt in the well-dressed group, Nancy declined. "I'd better wash off the sand before I sit down," she said.

"There are worse things than a little sand," Kostas commented wryly, and as she met his eyes, Nancy saw a gleam of amusement at the obvious reference to the mud episode of the night before.

Next to him, Loukia was looking at her with a peculiar light in her eyes, a look that made Nancy feel slightly uncomfortable.

"Nancy, please sit with us," Niko said. There was an urgency in his voice making her aware that in this situation he needed her. Remembering his overly sensitive feelings about Loukia, she accepted the offered chair.

The guests sat a long time over their coffee and rolls. At first Nancy found Loukia's conversation bright and witty. She had amusing anecdotes to tell about all sorts of celebrities, and her conversation was liberally sprinkled with clever side comments that set everyone laughing. Shortly, however, Nancy grew bored with talk of who was seeing whom, who was traveling where and who was wearing what. Yet the others seemed to be held spellbound by Loukia's quick and silvery laughter as she theatrically used her long manicured hands to emphasize a point. Looking around at their faces, Nancy noticed that even Kostas seemed charmed. The intense man who could discuss his nationalistic feelings so passionately seemed to her eyes to have become just another indolent man of the world.

Loukia's hand rested possessively on Kostas's arm, and Nancy could not help but admire the picture they made. Two sleek and beautiful creatures from another world than the one she lived in, they exuded a sense of power, perfect control and self-confidence. In the presence of those two handsome people, the closeness of the previous night, when she and Kostas had trudged together in the rain, paled into insignificance.

Suddenly, Nancy felt quite ordinary and wished herself anywhere but where she was. She would have got up at once if she didn't have a half-eaten roll on her plate and a newly refilled cup of steaming coffee before her. To excuse herself after barely touching her breakfast would seem strange indeed. And besides, Niko was unusually silent, and she could read the signs of a childhood storm brewing that would require her foresight to head off.

The boy's large eyes were sad and his thoughts seemed far away. She had never seen him like this and knew it was because of Loukia's presence. Yet Kostas's fiancée was perfectly charming to him, frequently addressing remarks to him that he would barely answer, instead mumbling and looking away. For the most part, however, he was ignored by the group, caught up in its own lighthearted chatter.

She was about to tactfully suggest to Niko that they excuse themselves and prepare for the morning's exercises, when Martin again turned his attention to her.

"I noticed you out on the beach when I was coming down to breakfast and I was filled with admiration! We of a sedentary disposition envy the more athletic. Do you jog every day? Perhaps I'll join you one morning, if the fresh air won't kill me." He patted his well-fed stomach ruefully.

"Every day I can," Nancy replied, charmed by his interest. "I find running increases my energy. But of course this is a wonderful spot for any outdoor activity." She gestured toward the beach and the blue sea beyond. "I'll be glad to run with you."

"Nancy *is* most athletic," Kostas commented in an amused tone, pouring coffee into his cup from a carafe, "she has energy enough for two."

Loukia turned a glittering smile on Kostas. "Americans are so very energetic! And always in such a hurry. I wonder, do they know how to enjoy life?" She lowered her eyes and speared a piece of melon with her fork. "It would appear from her lovely suntan and jogging that Nancy's nursing duties are well below her energy level. I am sure that in her place, working all day, I would be much too exhausted for exercise!"

Perhaps it was merely the minor language barrier that caused Nancy to sense an unkind insinuation, for Loukia's face remained friendly and her smile as bright as ever.

"Yes," Kostas said, breaking off a piece of roll and buttering it. "Nancy is a girl of many talents. She is an avid hiker and a skin diver as well."

"Oh?" Loukia arched a perfectly shaped eyebrow. "How very interesting. Where in America do you come from?"

"I live in Connecticut, on the east coast."

"Yes, I have visited there, I believe. A pretty state, but quite cold in the winter, is it not? But I am surprised you have had the opportunity to skin-dive in Connecticut! You have no real ocean there, do you?"

"Kostas has taught her," Niko said suddenly, with more animation than he had shown all morning. "Kostas says Nancy will be a very fine skin diver. He says she is a natural athlete."

His childish pride in her was touching, and Nancy flushed at the unexpected praise she had received. Again she glanced toward Kostas, but he was calmly sipping his coffee without corroborating his brother's claim.

"How nice for you," Loukia responded, after the barest of pauses. "I do so admire athletic women." And with that, she turned away, and Nancy and Niko were once more pushed into the background as the talk went on around them.

Nancy leaned over to Niko. "What do you say we get started on our exercises?"

"Yes, that is a good idea," he responded eagerly, obviously relieved to have an excuse to leave the table.

As Nancy stood up, excusing herself to go and work with Niko, Kostas looked up. He inclined his dark head in her direction. As he met her eyes, Nancy felt for an instant the unspoken bond that had linked them together the previous night. Then as she looked at Loukia and the rest of the group, the feeling faded and was replaced by a sense that she was an outsider. It was they who were linked together by bonds of a common background and culture. And Kostas was right—she could never be one of them!

CHAPTER NINE

NIKO WAS STARING out of the window of the exercise room when Nancy, showered and changed, entered twenty minutes later.

"Just because you have guests doesn't mean you can skip work, young man," she said, trying by her gay tone to raise his flagging spirits.

"They are not my guests," Niko replied flatly.

He lay down on the exercise mat beneath the leg press Antonis had bought, and Nancy adjusted the weights.

"Now, now,"she chided cheerfully, "where is that famous Greek hospitality? You sound as grumpy as a New Yorker during rush hour!"

But Niko, for once, did not respond to her teasing. Instead, he silently and far more strenuously than usual turned his full attention to his exercises, vigorously pushing the weights up and down with his legs until beads of perspiration stood out on his forehead. Nancy insisted upon a rest.

"Niki, I think you're overdoing it. Come and take a break now."

"No, I feel fine."

She mimicked his pouting face. "With a face like that! That's not my Niko!"

Niko sighed and brought his legs down, then sat up. "I am sorry, Nancy. I am in a bad mood today. I did not mean to be rude to you."

Nancy sat beside him on the floor and ruffled his dark curls affectionately. "Want to talk about it?"

He shook his head. "There is no use telling you any more, Nancy. You did not believe me the first time." Then he burst out in a sudden rush of feeling. "But you see, don't you, how they are, how she is? I hate them."

"Niko," she said, shocked by the intensity of his emotion, "I'm surprised at you. After all the things you said about Loukia, I expected to meet a monster. And what do I find? A very beautiful and charming woman."

Niko's frown deepened into a scowl. "If you think that, then she has you fooled, too," he said. "She is very good at that. She even fools Kostas, but I know she is not kind nor good. She is not any of the things *you* are."

Nancy laughed, cupping his chin in her hand. "Niko, honestly. You mustn't compare us as if we were in some sort of competition. Loukia and I are two entirely different people with different good and bad points. She must have many fine qualities—otherwise your brother wouldn't be engaged to her."

Niko shook his head vehemently. "Kostas is very smart. He is the smartest man I know. But about her he knows nothing. He does not see that she thinks only of herself."

He slumped down, his face a perfect study in misery. His feelings about Loukia were very negative, yet from what Nancy had seen there was no rational basis for his bias. Therefore there must be something else at the bottom of his overreaction.

He sighed, turning a face filled with sadness toward her. "He will be ruined by her," he said.

"Niko, please listen to me," she answered, beginning to suspect he was reacting out of a jealous fear that he was about to be displaced in his brother's affections. "Your brother and you are very dear friends. Your friendship won't be changed by his marriage to Loukia."

"You are wrong," the boy interrupted, refusing to be soothed by her words. "Everything will be different when they are married. Loukia does not like Korpas. She will want to live in Athens so that she can go to parties and be with her friends. And when I am in school I will have to live there with her. It will be terrible.''

"But you forget that your brother will also be living with you, and you'll have plenty of time with him.''

"Nancy, you do not know her. She does not like it when Kostas spends his time with me. She will do what she can to come between us.''

Nancy looked at him helplessly, sympathizing with his unhappiness. She was sure any woman Kostas had chosen would provoke the same response in him. He, of course, could not know that. She wished she knew how to reassure and help him.

"How wonderful it would be,'' he said wistfully as they resumed their exercises, "if you were to marry Kostas. You could stay here always and be my very own sister.''

His innocent remark touched her. Taking his hand, she said, "That's very sweet. There's nothing I'd like better than to stay here always and be your sister. But our relationship has nothing to do with Kostas.'' She folded the exercise mat and put it away. "You must trust him,'' she went on. "If he has chosen to marry Loukia, then you must believe it's the right decision. I'm sure Loukia will make your brother very happy.''

But Niko was in a rebellious mood and would not let her have the last word. "Real life is different from your American movies,'' he said scornfully, as if he were speaking to a child. "People who marry are not always right for each other. Kostas is blind about Loukia. He does not see that she can never make anyone happy.''

WHILE THE HOUSEHOLD SLEPT after lunch, Nancy wandered down to the beach with a book. She felt the need for solitude, to sort out the problem Niko had laid before her. Their talk had upset her, and she felt his confusion and unhappiness keenly. But she was puzzled about the best way to help him. Her heart went out to the boy, knowing from experience the terrible void his mother's death had left in his

young life. She was certain that his fierce attachment to her
and to Kostas was the direct result of that painful loss. It was
only natural that he believe he was about to lose a loved one
again, and out of that fear he had cast Loukia in the role of
villain. Matching Nancy and Kostas was Niko's childish at-
tempt to keep his loved ones securely by his side forever.

She placed her towel on the sand and stretched out, feeling the hot sun sinking into her bare back and legs. Poor
Niko, she thought. What a difficult time this was for him.
As if the loss of his mother years before and the terrible accident were not enough to cope with, now he was faced with
another major emotional upheaval.

The steady hiss of the waves soothed her and soon she felt
herself slipping into a half sleep, Niko's problems fading out
of consciousness. But just as she was about to drift off, she
felt a presence by her side. With a start she opened her eyes
to see Kostas standing next to her.

"I could not rest," he said, gesturing toward the house.
"There is something on my mind. I must speak to you."

Her heart stirred as he squatted down next to her and regarded her with a serious expression.

"What is it, Kostas?" she asked, wondering what to make
of his statement. There was a boyish appeal in his face that
made her feel she would agree to anything he might ask of
her.

"Tell me, Nancy," he said. "Has Niko spoken to you
about Loukia?"

She felt a pang of anxiety. Was this what he wanted to ask
her—about Niko and Loukia?

"What do you mean?" she asked, stalling for time, re-
luctant to reveal Niko's confidences, yet sensing that perhaps if Kostas were aware of the conflicts in Niko's mind he
might help the situation.

Kostas regarded her closely. "Niko refuses to speak to me
on the subject. Yet when Loukia is here, Niko behaves very
badly. You noticed it this morning, surely. And she had
bought him a very expensive gift, a jacket, for which he

barely thanked her. Loukia came to me before lunch, extremely upset. She was almost in tears, for she believes he does not like her. She is an openhearted person herself and becomes very hurt when others are rude to her.''

Nancy felt a surge of anger. Who was Kostas concerned about—Loukia or Niko? Feeling suddenly like Niko's self-appointed champion, she sat up and said, somewhat stiffly, "Niko has spoken to me. He doesn't like her.''

A shadow flickered across Kostas's face. He must really love Loukia, Nancy thought, to be so concerned about her feelings. If only he could transfer some of that concern to Niko.

"But," she added, feeling that perhaps she had spoken too bluntly, "I'm sure it's not because of Loukia. Niko feels insecure and jealous. He's afraid that he'll lose your love once you marry.''

"And do you believe he will?''

"No, of course not. But what I believe isn't important. Niko is at a very sensitive age, and his emotions run deep. He is entering adolescence. It can be a particularly painful time of life.''

Kostas's eyes darkened. "But he must accept things the way they are," he snapped. "I have told you this before. I would appreciate it if you would stop making excuses for what is, in the end, simply bad manners on his part. You must speak to him, make him see that he ought to be more polite to Loukia. She will, after all, soon be his sister-in-law.''

"But Kostas," Nancy protested, resenting his tone and the casual way he ordered her to deal with Niko's feelings. "Why don't *you* speak to him? Coming from you, I'm sure it would mean more.''

"You mean, no doubt," he replied with sarcasm, "that you do not believe he should respect my fiancée." He stood and smoothed out his linen slacks impatiently.

"No," she responded vehemently. "That is not true. I think he *ought* to be polite to Loukia. It's only that—''

"Good!" he interrupted brusquely. "We are agreed. You will speak to him soon. I do not want him upsetting Loukia when we are all together at the wine festival."

For a moment she met his gaze forcefully, still wanting to refuse the unfair task. But then she sighed, remembering the hopeless battles they had fought. She could not win fighting him. At least this once she would acquiesce. Perhaps, after all, he was right.

She let her eyes drop. "Yes, Kostas," she murmured, "I'll do what I can."

His whole body seemed to relax and his face lit with a pleased smile. "You are very helpful, little one," he said, leaning down and running his finger along the curve of her cheek. "If you succeed in changing Niko's attitude toward Loukia, you will make me very happy."

With a jaunty wave, he headed back toward the house. Nancy watched him go, his lithe body returning up the path to the house, his back straight and head erect as if nothing could shake his self-confidence. She put a hand to her cheek, absently retracing the path his finger had traveled, her thoughts and emotions in a turmoil. So that was how he rewarded acquiescence, she thought, stifling a sudden resentment. She rose and walked to the water, staring out at the horizon.

The words she had used earlier to Niko came back to her. "Loukia will make your brother happy," she had reassured him. And just now Kostas had said, "If you change Niko's mind, you will make me very happy."

Happy. All at once an overpowering sadness swept over her. She seemed to see Kostas's face as it had been just last night, inches from her own—the chiseled features, the intense dark eyes and sensual mouth. She unconsciously hugged her body as if she were cold. What would it mean to make Kostas happy? Then she pictured his face relaxed and happy as it had been during the dance the night of the anniversary party. The shining and open look had transformed him so that she had responded with a surge of joy of her own.

The thought came to her suddenly that no woman could ask more from life than to be the one to make him happy.

NIKO WAS AWAKE but still in bed when she looked in on him the next morning. He looked pale, and large dark circles ringed his eyes.

"Niko, honey, what is it?" Nancy asked in alarm.

"Nothing too bad. I think I have a cold. I feel very tired this morning, and my legs are begging me for a rest. They say to me, if you love us you will ask Nancy to let us stay in bed today."

It crossed her mind that perhaps he was feigning illness in order to avoid spending the day in Loukia's company. She sat down beside him and felt his forehead. He was somewhat cold to her touch, but not severely so. He probably was coming down with a cold, in which case a day of rest would be a good idea. She would stay at home with him and recommend that he not go to the wine festival that night.

Satisfied he was not seriously ill, she plumped up his pillows and headed for the kitchen.

She found Kiki unusually busy setting food into plastic containers, which she then packed into a large wicker hamper on the floor. Enough food for an army was out on the kitchen table.

Kiki greeted Nancy affectionately, stopping to wipe her brow with a handkerchief.

"Kiki, what in the world is going on?"

"Miss Loukia wishes to have a picnic." She poured Nancy some coffee, then sat down at the table and leaned a weary head against her arms. "She come to me early, very early, to say I must make food enough for a big party. If only she say something to me yesterday, I would have two girls in from the town to help."

Nancy got up and put an arm around the little woman's shoulders. "Oh, Kiki, let me help you."

"No, no," she said vehemently. "Kiki is very strong. She will make everything perfect for the guests."

But Nancy insisted on helping, and soon the basket was filled to overflowing with good food. No simple sandwiches, as were traditional for picnics in the United States, but salad, cold chicken and lamb and fresh loaves of bread—a feast.

It was pleasant working with Kiki. Nancy had nearly forgotten the confused feelings of the day before and her promise to speak to Niko, when Kostas came through the outside door with wine and beer he had purchased in town.

"Put these in the basket as well, Kiki," he ordered. "I had a hard time finding any wine shops open—everyone is preparing for the festival."

Then his attention turned to Nancy. "Now, Nancy, you must bring your swimming suit and a jacket, for we're going in the motorboat and might not return until late afternoon."

"I didn't realize I was coming along on your picnic, Kostas."

"Nonsense. Get Niko up and tell him to get dressed at once. We're leaving in thirty minutes."

"Niko has a slight cold this morning," Nancy said. "He ought to stay in and rest today, and I think I should stay here with him."

Kostas's brows came together in a frown, and he looked at Nancy with suspicion. "Has he said he wishes to remain home?"

"Yes."

"Then if he is resting, there will not be much you can do for him. Let Kiki care for him. You have not been to this part of the island, and I know you will find it beautiful."

"I really think I ought to be here," she said, feeling she had a duty to stay with the boy and not go chasing off on an outing, no matter how much fun it might be.

"Declare a holiday. Niko is not a baby," he answered curtly. "Surely you do not think one afternoon alone will harm him."

Before Nancy could reply, a musical voice interrupted from the doorway. "Nancy is quite right, Kostas. We must not interfere. Of course it is better that she remain with Niko. She is his nurse, after all."

Although Loukia's voice sounded thoughtful and sympathetic enough, Nancy saw with a start how coldly impersonal the eyes were when they met hers. It probably was a reflection of Loukia's feelings toward those not of her class, Nancy thought, judging from the way she treated poor Kiki, expecting her to prepare a feast on a moment's notice.

"Loukia is right, Kostas," Nancy said. "What if Niko should need me?"

"It is time you stopped babying Niko. I'll expect you down in twenty minutes." And with that he turned on his heel and marched out, Loukia following behind him, the hem of her white morning gown dusting the floor.

Yes, your Highness, Nancy thought, resisting the impulse to bow in mock obedience. She had never been ordered to a picnic before. She stood there staring after the pair, wondering what to make of such a command. Why, he might as well order her to have a good time!

Kiki touched her elbow gently. "Do as Kostas tells you, Nancy. He knows what is best."

Nancy turned to her, puzzled. How was it that Kostas inspired such loyalty and obvious affection from the little servant when, as far as she could tell, Kiki had been treated discourteously by him?

"You like Kostas very much, don't you, Kiki?" she asked, beginning to slip the cold bottles into the spaces of the picnic basket.

Kiki's homely face lit with pleasure. "Yes." She nodded her head so vigorously that her little dark curls bobbed up and down as if on springs. "He is a most wonderful man, for he does many things for my family. When my mother was sick, Kostas paid for the doctor, and he took her to the hospital for the operation. Also, Kostas has made it possible for my nephew, Dimitri, to go to the university. Kostas—he is like my own son."

The servant frowned at Nancy's disbelieving expression. "Sometimes he seems not so kind, yes?"

"Yes," Nancy replied.

"I know Kostas all his life, since he was a small boy when I came to work for his mama. Believe Kiki, he is a good man. You will see."

THE BOAT BOUNDED across the swells to the east side of the island. Nancy enjoyed the sting of salt spray blowing at her as she sat in the stern. Loukia sat close to Kostas, her shoulder touching his. Every now and then the Greek woman would raise an elegantly manicured hand to brush away a lock of his hair that had blown across his forehead. Each time she did so, Nancy averted her gaze, feeling uncomfortable. It was as if she were an intruder on a private scene.

Soon a rocky island appeared about two miles off, and Kostas swung the boat around and headed toward it. The sea was rough once they were out of the shelter of Korpas. Nancy had to hold on tight to the side, while Loukia's friends huddled in a group, clinging to one another and making much laughter and noise. They slid easily from one language to another and at last, French and Italian and Greek having been temporarily exhausted, they turned to English.

"There's no water on it, darling," a girl named Katina said shrilly. "How do you expect us to live there without water?"

"I suppose not that particular island, then," answered a slight slim-waisted boy with the ponderous name of Socrates. "But there must be some spot on earth where we can all live together and do exactly as we please, away from established notions of morality."

"What, and be stuck with one another day in and day out with nothing to do? I'd die of boredom."

"I don't see what would be different about that," said the young man sitting closest to Nancy in an angry voice. "You're all dying of boredom, anyway. None of you do anything. You're all a bunch of parasites, living off your families."

"Theo is starting up again," Katina warned, her merry laugh cascading over the sound of the engine. "Theo, I don't see that your poems make you any better than the rest of us. They're not very good. Besides, your parents are supporting you, as well."

"What do you know about it?" Theo retorted bitterly, scowling out toward the water.

"Well, now," Martin's voice boomed with heartiness, "we're not exactly as degenerate as you would like to believe, Theo. We do have, among us, at least two contributing members of society. Just thinking about all that Kostas does in one day exhausts me." He gave a self-deprecating laugh. "Why, I haven't worked since mother married the colonel. And look at Nancy here. She's doing something with her life. I daresay she's never bored."

"Martin, really," Loukia drawled, "you are so tiresome. Why must you take the fun out of Theo's little game?"

They lapsed into silence until Loukia changed the subject. "What do you think about having supper at home?" she asked the group. "Kiki can prepare something light before we go to town for the festival."

"But I thought we'd decided to eat in town," Katina said.

Loukia turned around and arched one perfect brow in mock horror. "Darling, these island restaurants are so filthy! No, we'll do better if we eat something at home. I'll tell Kiki when we return."

Poor Kiki, Nancy thought, imagining the little woman waiting on Niko and then having to prepare yet another meal for the large group. The evening meal was always small, yet Nancy knew Kiki would put herself out for the guests. Had she known Loukia was planning more work for Kiki, Nancy would have insisted on staying at the house to help.

Then the talk switched to clothes, with Katina insisting that only in Paris could one buy truly elegant clothes. Loukia disagreed, as it seemed to Nancy she did at every point in the discussion today.

"Paris has had her day," Loukia objected. "The big couturiers are passé. Rome and London and even Madrid have the truly exciting designers."

"Then there is America," Katina said. "Halston, and..."

Loukia's delicate features twisted into a sneer of disdain. "Katina," she sighed in despair. "What do they know of fashion in America besides—" she shuddered "—jeans and T-shirts."

Briefly, Nancy wondered if the cutting comment were aimed at her. After all, she frequently wore jeans and T-shirts. But of course, she told herself, Loukia had no cause for hostility toward her. The comment must have been unthinking rather than personally insulting.

She was relieved when Loukia continued the conversation in Greek. Now she could tune out gracefully, spared the seemingly endless chatter. She had quickly grown tired of their idle gossip and began to wonder if Niko hadn't been right in his assessment.

How could Kostas bear it, she wondered, taking a look at him as he sat with a straight back, steering the boat. He had shown himself to have a deeper side to his personality; he was interested in more serious matters. How could he enjoy the company of people who never seemed to have anything more on their minds than their own pleasure?

And as for Loukia, beautiful as she undeniably was, she seemed, judging from this brief exposure, not to share anything more substantial with him than a common culture. Still, she thought as the boat flung white spray at her, there must be more to Loukia than her glib conversation revealed. For why else would Kostas have chosen her for his fiancée?

As the boat cut through the sea, the rocky island toward which they were headed loomed larger and larger, a pale-pink color against the azure sky and darker blue water. Kostas skillfully maneuvered the boat between boulders, and finally they were clambering out into shallow, crystal-clear water, leaving the boat anchored behind them.

There wasn't much of a beach here, but an easy climb brought them to a smooth shelf of rock, obviously once a beach but now considerably above water level. Here the sunbathers spread their blankets and towels. Loukia stretched out her bronzed limbs and unwound her turban, revealing a beautifully arranged and elaborate coiffure.

"Who will go diving?" Kostas asked after he set the heavy basket down in their midst.

"Not me, *cara*," Loukia drawled. "I've just done my hair and I want it to last until the wine festival. I wouldn't dare get it wet."

No one else seemed interested in moving a muscle. Only Nancy, who hadn't had either her run or a workout with Niko, was longing for some physical exercise.

She felt torn. Some instinct warned her she mustn't offer to go. Loukia's possessive behavior toward Kostas suggested that she was not the kind of woman who would take lightly to the idea of her fiancé spending time alone with another woman. So, instead of responding to Kostas's query, she spread her towel on the sand and lay down, closing her eyes.

"I can always count on one energetic soul," she heard Kostas say. Her heart lurched painfully against her ribs at his words. "Nancy, come with me," he said.

Opening her eyes, she saw him standing over her, a slight smile playing over his lips. She wanted to go very much.

She pushed aside the warning that repeated itself in her mind that Loukia could be a treacherous enemy. *She* knew there was nothing wrong in her relationship with Kostas, and therefore no reason for Loukia to object.

"Why not?" she said, hoping he could not see the warm flush she felt spreading over her face. She took the hand he offered and let him pull her to her feet.

Loukia raised her head and peered at Nancy from behind her dark glasses. Nancy had the impression that she was regretting her coiffure.

"Do stay and keep us company, Nancy," Loukia said in syrupy tones. "Kostas is not Niko. He can fend for himself."

"Can't you see the girl is dying for a swim?" Martin interjected. "Don't worry, Loukia, she'll bring Kostas safely back."

Loukia shot Martin a withering glance. Nancy could feel the hostility as she picked up her beach bag and followed Kostas to the shore. By now she knew full well that by going with Kostas she had incurred Loukia's wrath, yet she was delighted to escape the woman's company and spend time at a favorite activity. And Kostas himself seemed as unruffled as ever, making Nancy wonder if he had noticed Loukia's dig at her and Martin's clever rejoinder.

She had been practicing with the snorkel on her afternoons alone, and after a few uncomfortable incidents in which she breathed in water and came up coughing and sputtering, she had learned to dive with it. She now had the mask, fins and snorkel in her bag and intended to surprise Kostas by diving for real.

The beach fell away steeply, and soon they were in the water up to their waists.

"Do not go far," Kostas ordered. "You are safe here, where it is shallow. I will return shortly." Then he disappeared beneath the surface.

Nancy stood by herself for several moments and then, confident of her newly acquired ability, she adjusted her mask and dove beneath the surface, intending to follow him. In a few moments she found herself in deeper water. It was mysterious and a little frightening. She looked around for Kostas, but he wasn't in sight.

Fear tightened her throat. She suddenly felt very vulnerable, all alone in the unpopulated underwater world. Kostas had disappeared into the shadowy depths as if he had never been with her at all. She kicked up to the surface and drew in a deep shaky breath of air. Maybe she ought to stay where he had said, on the surface in shallow water. At least there was no danger near the shore.

But she was not one to back away from a challenge. She had to shake herself out of her fear by diving again, by taking a deep breath and then seeing how far she could go. Her legs were strong enough to swim all around the island, if necessary. There was no reason she couldn't master this new skill.

She dove again and found a path between speckled boulders thick with algae. Conquering her fear, she went through it and came out into a sunny shallow lagoon that ended in a smooth curve of pink rock at the base of the island.

It was a moment of triumph when she saw Kostas sitting on the rocks, his fins beside him and his mask pushed up off his face. He had caught several fish and was stringing them onto a nylon line.

Her heart leaped at the sight of him.

"This island is excellent for fishing," he shouted to her, waving his catch exuberantly. "No one comes to frighten the fish. They virtually leap onto my spear."

She swam up to the rocks and pulled herself up beside him.

"So," he said, looking her over as she removed her mask, "you disobeyed me and dove?" She expected him to be angry with her as he had been the day she had gone hiking into the hills and injured her shoulder, and she steeled herself for a lecture. But instead of disapproval, he looked at her proudly.

"And how did it seem to you, this strange landscape beneath the waves? You were a little frightened, I think. I see it on your face."

"I was a little," she admitted. "But it isn't really dangerous if you know what you're doing and you're a strong swimmer. I don't think it will be long before Niko can dive with you again."

Kostas's face darkened. "Yes," he said, "if he hasn't lost his nerve." He squinted out toward the horizon, which was blue and flat, then back at her. "You know, of course, that it was a diving accident that almost killed Niko?"

"Yes, but Niko never talked about it, and so I don't know any of the details. How did it happen?"

"He was diving in the harbor with some other boys. He was beneath the surface and failed to notice a fishing boat coming in with its catch. He came up in front of it and had no time to get out of the way. We—my father and I—thought it was all over for him. He was broken like a little toy."

Suddenly he turned to face her, and all traces of the good humor of a few moments ago were gone. "Why did you not let the boy come today?" he demanded. "I saw him before we left. I do not believe he is ill. He had no fever. He could have dressed warmly and then sat with the others in the sun. You behave as if he is still sick, yet you tell me he is almost ready to dive."

He brought his fist down flat against the rock. "By God, I believe you have created a permanent invalid. By letting him stay in bed and then telling him you will remain there to wait on him, you teach him to indulge his weakness! Remember, I told you there is no room for weakness here. If Niko is to be a cripple, at least let him be a strong one!"

Startled at Kostas's change of tone, Nancy felt a surge of anger. Once again he was challenging her professional judgment.

"No room for weakness?" she repeated, bursting back at him. "Your notions about Niko and the hard life on this island seem to be confused, Kostas. You lecture me as if I were a soft and pampered child, yet you yourself live in the lap of luxury. Did it ever occur to you that I know more of the hard life than you ever will? I didn't inherit a fortune. I didn't grow up with adoring servants to cater to my every whim! Every single thing I've accomplished I've earned myself!''

"Yes?'' he responded, a cynical sneer distorting his features. "I am very aware of your so-called struggles. And isn't it my father's offer that made Niko so appealing to you?'' His harsh laugh cut into her. "It is so clear to me,'' he continued, "that I wonder how you believe anyone else could be fooled! When in your life could you expect to be paid twice your normal salary, or to live in a house such as ours? And who knows where your ambition is headed!''

So there it was, out in the open. This was why he resented her so much; not simply because she was a foreigner, as Panos had implied, but because somewhere inside he suspected that she had her eyes on him.

"That's unfair,'' she retorted, although she knew it was hopeless. Nothing she could say would cause him to alter his opinion of her. "I love Niko as if he were my own brother, not because your father is giving me money.''

"But Niko is not your brother. Soon you will leave him and never see him again. Whatever else we can say about you, your affection has been bought.''

Stung, Nancy could only stare at him. He had seemed to utter the words with deliberate cruelty, his dark eyes blazing at her. With a sinking sensation in the pit of her stomach, she realized that Kostas honestly believed her attempts at friendship were motivated by opportunism.

The unfairness and savagery of his attack, which had come so unexpectedly, left her reeling. She felt bitterly hurt and longing for revenge.

"And when I leave, and you and Loukia marry,'' she hissed furiously without thinking of what she was saying, only wanting to inflict pain, "Niko will have a sister he despises. I'm glad you're so concerned about your brother, Kostas!"

Pain seemed to sear her chest as he turned from her with an angry utterance.

"There is one thing I see quite clearly," she continued, braver now that he wasn't looking directly at her with those snapping eyes. "You say you must marry a Greek woman so you can be sure of her. But have you taken a good look at your future wife? She's extremely beautiful and charming, but she won't swim because she's afraid to get her hair wet. She won't eat in town because the restaurants aren't clean enough. Is she the 'tough' woman who's accustomed to hardship? If you can't see the disparity between your grand words and your actions, then you are either the biggest hypocrite or the biggest fool I have ever met!"

He turned back to her again, and his eyes had softened. A trace of a smile formed on his lips. "You are not jealous, Nancy?"

"Certainly not!" All of a sudden she felt an intense desire to get away from that mocking smile. She tried to wriggle down to where she could plunge back into the water, but Kostas stopped her. He put a large hand on her wet head and brought her face close to his. She tried to pull away, but he mastered her easily.

She began to struggle, crying, "Kostas, let me go," but his free hand went up over her mouth, silencing her. She felt like a trapped animal, fighting to free herself.

"Hush, little one. Don't speak. Don't spoil pleasure with words." His arms went around her, pulling her tightly against his chest. Then his lips were on hers, hot and salty from the sea and sun. She felt herself yielding. Her head was tilted back and the sun beat on her closed eyelids. Her lips opened under his assault, and she felt his tongue against hers.

A surge of joy swept through her at his ardor. He wants me, she thought. He wants *me*, not Loukia! And for the moment, wanting him with an intensity she had never thought to experience, she forgot the harsh words they had just exchanged, forgot all the reasons why she should not be kissing him. She gave herself up to his embrace.

It seemed as if hours had passed, but it was only a minute or two. Nancy brought her hands up to touch his damp hair, felt for the first time his skin under her hands, bringing her fingers to his ears, to the hinge of his jaw, around to his throat where the pulse throbbed against her fingertips. It was as if her hands had a life of their own. They acted as though they had done this many times before, yet they had never before touched a man in this intimate, passionate, seeking way.

Suddenly the spell was broken by a splash, and they both broke away in time to see Kostas's fish and the line disappearing beneath the water.

Kostas laughed and leaned toward her again. He gave her a quick hard kiss, then plunged into the water and disappeared after his catch.

Alone on the rock, Nancy had time to think. She knew she ought to regret what had happened, but she wasn't at all sorry, for now she realized how much she had longed to kiss him ever since the night they had walked to the temple in the moonlight. The memory of her arguments with him faded into insignificance with the glorious knowledge that he wanted her.

The sunlight dancing on the water seemed the most pleasing sight in the world. She counted the seconds until he would emerge from the depths and look at her with love in his dark eyes and a happy smile she had longed to see on his face.

She was brutally disappointed when he emerged from the water with a face closed to her once more.

"You must forget what happened between us," he said as he gathered his fins and mask from beside her.

She could feel the blood drain out of her face. What kind of insensitive monster was he, she thought, that he could take her in his arms and kiss her with such feeling, then a moment later act as if she mattered to him less than a fish?

Hurt and anger once more gathered force within her. "It was nothing," she retorted in the iciest of tones, forcing back her tears. A strangely hurt expression crossed his face briefly, and Nancy was glad to find a way to hurt him.

His expression hardened and closed. "You have spoken the truth," he said harshly. "Kissing you that way was a mistake, and I never make the same mistake twice. Now come down from the rocks. The others will be having lunch."

The water seemed icy cold to her, and she had no feeling in her arms and legs as she followed him toward the beach. Even when they got out into the hot sun and climbed the path to the rocky ledge, her teeth were chattering.

Loukia met them with a smile that seemed a bit too glittering. She was removing the contents of the basket, taking each item and setting it on the blanket with deliberation, as if she were afraid she'd break one of her scarlet nails if she moved faster.

"Kostas, my sweet," she purred, "you must be tired and hungry. Come here and let me give you some food." She turned to her friends. "I do believe a woman should cater to her man, not try to compete with him. Don't you agree, Katina? Kostas, you must sit by me and drink your beer."

Kostas stripped off his diving suit and went to sit beside Loukia as she had said. Nancy watched him take a morsel of food from her fingers with his lips and wash it down with a swallow of beer. She felt slightly sick. How she wished she had remained here with the others after all. Had she obeyed her inner voice, she and Loukia might now be friendly, and Kostas would not have been able to hurt her so.

When Nancy went to the basket to take some food, Loukia looked her over from behind her dark glasses.

"American men like athletic women, I suppose," she commented to no one in particular as her eyes took in Nancy's slender but strongly muscled legs. "But then the women rule the home over there, I understand."

Nancy felt herself color at this very clear barb, and in her consternation, she dropped an olive into the dirt.

"Thank goodness," Loukia went on with a little laugh, "in civilized countries a woman is still a woman." She ran her fingertips along Kostas's bare leg. "And a man a man."

Heaven help Kostas, Nancy thought as the truth of Niko's assessment came home to her. She returned to her towel with tears burning beneath her eyelids, knowing exactly what kind of a woman Loukia Kassandras was.

Heaven help Kostas for choosing this woman to be his wife, she said to herself. Then, thinking again of his degrading treatment of her, she thought, *perhaps they are two of a kind and they deserve each other.*

Strangely that thought was no comfort, and the piece of bread she was trying to chew felt as if it would choke her.

CHAPTER TEN

NANCY STRIPPED OFF her clothes and stepped into the shower, trying to relax under the warm spray, hoping she could somehow cleanse herself of this afternoon and its humiliation.

The whole household, with the exception of Niko and herself, planned to drive into town together for the festival after supper. She knew the boy wanted to go very much, but he was still not looking well when she returned from the picnic, and she decided that it would be best for him to continue to rest.

Nancy, too, had been looking forward to the evening, never having been to a wine festival before and welcoming any chance to see more of the island customs. But the thought of spending more time in Loukia's company, having to hold her tongue while feeling herself the object of the woman's derision, was repugnant to her.

Yet with her usual honesty, Nancy had to admit to herself that her dampened enthusiasm was based on more than just dislike for Loukia. She could still feel the burning pressure of Kostas's lips on hers and the sensual way her body had responded. It was Kostas's company, even more than Loukia's, that she wanted to avoid.

The shower refreshed her tired body but did little to renew her spirits. As she dried herself with a thick towel, she could hear cheerful voices from outside her window as the others had cocktails on the veranda. Unconsciously her ear strained for sounds of Kostas's voice, and when she heard his rich laughter it was as though a knife had plunged into her heart. Wearily she shut the double door, wishing she could shut out her feelings as easily as the sounds.

She slipped into a white cotton caftan and went down the hall to Niko's room, hoping to catch him before supper. The boy was dressing slowly, a gloomy expression on his face.

"Niko, what is it? Why are you out of bed?"

He turned a wan smile on her. "I do not understand my brother," he said. "He has changed, Nancy. I have never known him this way."

"What happened? What did he say to you?" she asked, a fierce maternalism arising in her at his words.

"Kiki asked me if I would like to take my supper in my room. I said I would like that. But Kostas became very angry and ordered me to eat with the others. Nancy, why would he force me to sit at the table with Loukia when she makes me so unhappy?"

Nancy was silent for a moment. She had promised to talk to Niko, and now he had given her the perfect opening. Yet after this afternoon, could she say things to him she didn't believe any longer? She would have to find a way to convey Kostas's message.

Sinking into the easy chair by the French doors, she told him, "Perhaps Kostas feels hurt by you."

"Hurt by me? But I would never hurt him! I would do anything in the world for him."

"I think he feels you don't like Loukia. But he's going to marry her, so he must love her very much." The words almost stuck in her throat. "Can you imagine how you would feel if your very own brother didn't like someone you loved?"

The boy's face took on a strange expression. He stood, hands on hips, a frown of concentration on his face. "Yes, I can imagine," he replied at last.

"I'm sure, Niko," she continued, carefully saying what she knew to be true and leaving out her own judgments, "that if you were friendlier to Loukia, Kostas would no longer be angry with you."

There was truth in what she said, but it was a half truth and therefore dangerous. She resented bitterly being forced into collusion with Kostas, feeling as she did about Loukia. In keeping her promises to Kostas, she was committing an injustice to Niko. After all, why should Niko, a child, be made to feel responsible for the way his brother treated him? Good relations between the two of them had always been Kostas's responsibility, simply because he was so much older.

Although she wished that her words didn't carry such weight with Niko, she saw that her argument had convinced him. He came over to her with a new expression in his eyes, a look of maturity, she thought, as though he had understood far more than what she actually had said.

"Yes," he told her seriously. "You are quite right, Nancy. I can see that Kostas might be hurt by my feelings toward Loukia. That is how I feel because of the way Kostas treats you. You are my friend and yet he is unfriendly to you. I see I have upset my brother, and I will try to be nicer to Loukia. Perhaps she will be nicer to me, after all, and maybe then he will also become kind to you."

Nancy was stunned by the unexpected parallel Niko had drawn. She hadn't realized that the antagonism between Kostas and herself had been evident enough for Niko to perceive.

She wanted to take his dear little head and hold it against her breast, but she knew that would be a mistake. He was a man at the moment, and growing more mature all the time. Kostas had been right about one thing—she must not hold him back, must not try to keep him a little boy. She would have to let him go, let him take more responsibility for himself. But not, she thought angrily as she left the room, by withdrawing love and support, no matter what Kostas thought best!

Still clad in the thin caftan, Nancy made her way along the hall to the kitchen. She wanted to check with Kiki to see if she could have her dinner in her room. She had no intention of joining the others on the veranda this evening. She had had more than enough of their company for one day.

Pungent aromas greeted her. Kiki was feverishly active, scurrying from sink to counters, pantry to stove in order to prepare the evening meal.

"Nancy!" she exclaimed, her homely face crinkled in pleasure. "What can Kiki do for you?"

"Not a thing, Kiki." Nancy gestured toward the oven. "What is it that smells so wonderful?"

Kiki's smile widened even further, showing two gold teeth. "*Moussaka*—lamb and eggplant together. Very good."

"Kiki," Nancy said, "if it's not too much trouble, I'd like to take my dinner back up to my room later. I won't join the others."

The servant's eyes widened in concern. "You are not well? It is your arm that is troubling you?"

Nancy flushed, unable, in the face of the woman's obvious concern, to lie. "It's not exactly that, Kiki. Only I don't wish to go to the festival tonight after all—"

"And why is that?" a deep voice interrupted.

Nancy turned around quickly to see Kostas towering in the doorway, an empty ice bucket in one hand. At once, Kiki hurried to take the bucket from him. Kostas was regarding her so closely that Nancy felt naked. Instinctively, she clutched the loose-fitting caftan closer to her body.

"And why is it you have decided to deprive us of your company tonight?" Kostas's eyes held a glint of amusement, or was it mockery?

"I don't feel well," she stammered, "and I thought . . ."

Kostas took a step toward her and placed his hand on her forehead. Nancy's knees trembled at his touch, her cheeks burning at the memory of his passionate embrace.

"Another invalid!" he said sarcastically. "It is a strange illness you and Niko share. Neither of you is feverish. Why is it you wish to eat alone in your room and miss the festival?"

Feeling absurdly like a schoolgirl caught in a lie, she briefly wondered if he would order her to supper as he had so unfairly done to Niko. "If you must know, I don't have anything appropriate to wear," she answered lamely, hating herself for the dishonesty, yet knowing any excuse was better than telling Kostas the truth about why she didn't want to be in his presence—tonight or any other night.

Kostas continued to survey her with a gleam of ironic humor in his eyes. "This is a small-town festival," he remarked wryly, "not the opening of the opera in New York! I have seen you wear several outfits that are most becoming."

Conscious of Kiki's bright eyes on them, Nancy mustered all her dignity and pulled herself up to her full height, nevertheless feeling ridiculous under Kostas's close scrutiny.

"I came here prepared to work, not go to parties."

"Then consider the festival part of your duties," Kostas responded curtly. "Because you are going to accompany Niko tonight."

Stung by the sudden command, she couldn't stop herself from responding bitterly. "Neither Niko nor I is here on earth for your convenience," she snapped

Kostas flung back his head in the same impatient gesture he had used the morning he had tried to order her into his car.

"You are a most contrary woman," he muttered. "I have asked you more than once not to coddle Niko, and what do you do? You keep him indoors because of a cold that only you can see. I have asked you, please, to talk with Niko about his treatment of Loukia, and he is still doing his best to insult her. But this time I will not ask you to respect my wishes. I will order you, for I can see that is the only way to handle a woman as stubborn as you. This time, Nancy, you must do as I say, or I will send you packing!"

"That's what you've wanted to do from the beginning, isn't it?" she flung back. "You never wanted your father to bring me here at all."

His face grew dark, his eyebrows forming a threatening black line across his forehead. "Get dressed," he ordered. "We are leaving at eight o'clock. If you are not ready, I will carry you from your room naked."

He snatched the newly filled ice bucket from Kiki and stalked out of the kitchen.

Trembling, Nancy turned back to Kiki to find the little servant standing and staring with wide eyes. *"Den katalaveno,"* she said, shrugging and looking toward the ceiling.

"What, Kiki? What don't you understand?"

The servant shook her head. "I do not understand you. Why do you speak so to him? And Kostas—I have never seen him this way. It is not right, this trouble between a man and a woman." Pursing her lips, she busied herself once more with her cooking.

Nancy slipped back into her room and began contemplating her clothes closet. *Does he really think I'd make up an illness for Niko just to spite him,* she wondered. *And surely he could have let me have the evening to myself,* she thought as she pulled out a print dress with a pale yellow background and held it up to herself in the mirror. *He knows Niko needs only one responsible adult to look out for him.*

At any rate it was plain that she had no choice. She would have to go. And she was not about to be dragged out of her room naked, as Kostas had threatened.

She dressed quickly, looking in the mirror long enough to see that the dress brought out the best of her figure and that the bright color had even managed to lend a glow to her pale cheeks and tired, unhappy eyes. It was strictly a casual dress, but then as Kostas said, the occasion was hardly formal.

She sat at the table by her window and ate her tray of *moussaka* and salad, wondering a little sadly how Niko was enjoying his meal in the company of Loukia. Would he carry out his good intentions and be more diplomatic with her? And how would the Greek woman respond to his attentions? Would she be satisfied?

As Nancy was finishing her meal, she heard hurried steps on the floor outside her room, followed by a tapping on the door, Kiki stepped into the room, so loaded down with freshly laundered towels and clothes that only the top of her head was visible.

"Let me help you," Nancy said, taking the pile of sweet-smelling laundry and placing it on the bed.

"Oh, Nancy," Kiki sighed. "I am sorry to bring the clothes so late." She began to separate the laundry that belonged to Nancy from that of the others in the household.

"Why are you doing the wash at this hour, Kiki? Surely you can rest now that you've finished making supper?"

The servant sighed tragically, and her dark brows knit together in the closest that Nancy had ever seen her come to a frown. "The girls did not come today to help me, and I could not fold the laundry before this. When I have finished, I can eat and perhaps go to the festival."

"There must be a great deal of extra work for you," Nancy commiserated.

"I do not mind the work," Kiki said, her mouth set in a thin line. "I like work. All my life I work. But I do not like this 'Kiki, get me this,' 'Kiki, get me that.' All day there is one person who keeps me running. Nothing is right for her. The dress is not ironed good or the floor not dusted or the coffee not hot. I do not know what will happen when . . ."

She broke off and looked rather helplessly at Nancy. "But I do not wish to complain."

"That's all right, Kiki," Nancy said, comforting her. "I understand. And I'll put the clothes away for you. You go back to eat your supper."

Resolving to tell Kostas about how Kiki was overworked, she began putting the laundry in the proper drawers.

At a quarter to eight she was sitting in her chair trying to concentrate on an Agatha Christie novel Barbara had loaned her. She was nervous. Kostas had said he would come to get her at eight and carry her out, whether she was ready or not. Well, she decided, if he had a right to give orders, she had a right to be difficult. Not that she dared test him as far as dress was concerned, but she would show him just how stubborn she could be when she was under attack. She would sit in her room. Let him come after her!

Kostas didn't bother to knock. At 8:02 he flung open the door and stood in her room, his face a study of annoyance.

"You're two minutes late," Nancy said calmly, looking at her watch. "I've been ready for hours."

"You might have spared me the trouble and come to the car yourself," he snapped.

"Frankly, I wanted to find out what kind of man you are. Now I know you make good your threats. Fortunately, I saw fit to put some clothes on."

"It would not matter to me one way or the other," he replied acidly. "I will not have a servant—clothed or unclothed—who does not know how to behave properly. I said if you were not ill, you were to come, and that is what I meant."

"Servant!" she repeated bitterly. "Is that what I am?"

"What else?" He shrugged casually. "Come, the others are waiting."

She remained in her chair glowering at him. Servant indeed! Once again she felt an uncontrollable need to hurt him.

"I have news for you," she retorted. "You call me a servant, but you treat your servants like slaves. Slavery has been abolished in both our countries. I'm not your slave—and neither is Kiki, no matter what you and Loukia may think!"

His threatening look turned dangerous. He grabbed hold of her arm and yanked her to her feet. "Slavery?" he said derisively. "Is that what you call it? Kiki is as well paid as you. There are no slaves in the Paradissis house."

"No, I suppose not. You *buy* your slaves, or think you do. But someday Kiki will rebel, as I am doing now."

"Oh, is this a revolution?" He stood back, a sudden glint of amusement appearing on his face. "I don't believe I heard the manifesto. What is it you are rebelling against?"

"Against, among other things, Niko's being ordered to go to the festival against my better judgment. The child is ill, whether you believe it or not. And as for me, I'm a grown woman and have a perfect right to make decisons for myself."

"Yes, you are a woman," he replied, glancing down at the slender figure that looked unusually full in the yellow dress, "but not a very smart one. You seem better at making a man furious with you than giving him what he wants."

"And what is that? Absolute power over her, body and soul? Why should any woman grant you the right to treat her the way you do me?"

"Enough!" he thundered suddenly. She was sure everyone in the house could hear him. "Come now or I will not be responsible for my actions."

"Yes, I will come," she said with ice in her voice and narrowed eyes. "I'll do exactly as you tell me, though I have no idea why it's so important that I come at all."

She followed him out the door. "Surely you could look after Niko by yourself. Or do you just want him conveniently out of the way so he won't be any trouble?" Her voice bounced off the marble floor of the hall and echoed up the stairs.

Kostas stood still for a moment, looking astounded. "Certainly I could look after Niko," he replied more quietly. "But of course it is Niko who insisted that you come. Doesn't it please you that I am respecting his wishes?"

"You might have asked me instead of ordering me," she said after digesting this information. "I didn't have the slightest idea this was Niko's idea. Naturally I would have agreed to come had I known. He's my first consideration."

"This misunderstanding is your fault," he said. "If you had not offered me such an argument, I would certainly have—."

Suddenly a door closed above them, interrupting his explanation, and a slender figure in a flowing dress tripped gracefully down the stairs.

"Darling, where have you been?" Loukia said, reaching Kostas's side and taking hold of her arm possessively. "I was just looking for you in your room. We've all been waiting."

Nancy was sure, considering the way Kostas had been shouting and the fact that her door had been open the whole time, that Loukia knew exactly where he had been. But she was too angry to care whether or not Loukia had overheard their unpleasant exchange. Staring stonily ahead, Nancy headed for the door.

"I am coming now," Kostas answered Loukia. "Is Niko in the car?"

"Of course, Kostas," she purred. "He's been waiting so impatiently for you—just like the excitable boy he is."

She turned her brilliant eyes on Nancy. "Niko has been so charming tonight. I do think having people around is good for his disposition. A child should not be kept cooped up day and night, don't you agree?"

Before Nancy could reply, Loukia turned her attention back to Kostas. "Once we are married, we shall see to it he is no longer so sheltered."

Kostas closed and locked the door behind them, and they walked to the Mercedes. The other group had gone off earlier in a taxi.

Niko, who was looking much better, leaned out the window to call to her enthusiastically. "Nancy, are you coming after all? Hurry, come sit next to me!"

Resigned, she got in, but not without some bitter reflection. Not only had she been subjected to another exhausting fight with Kostas, but she now had an evening with Loukia and her friends to look forward to. Niko would be

with her, true enough, and there was every chance she'd see
Barbara and Panos. But these others—they depressed her.
All glitter and no substance, like fool's gold. Even Martin,
the only one who had shown the slightest bit of warmth, was
really no better than the others. Couldn't Kostas see them
for what they were?

She regarded Kostas's dark shape as he leaned forward to
start the engine. She wondered, turning to look out at the
darkening landscape, why Kostas's abruptness with her that
evening had become so explosive. And she, had she not been
especially quick to become angry with him? And all over a
silly misunderstanding. She had provoked him and tried to
hurt him, and she was as mystified by her own behavior as
by his.

The town was transformed. Throngs of gaily dressed
people filled the narrow streets, and lights gleamed from
every restaurant and *taverna*, reflecting on the dark water.
And everywhere there was the sound of the infectious Greek
music.

Nancy was glad she had worn her simple cotton dress,
even though the others in the party were decked out in expensive and elegant clothes. Loukia was stunning in her
well-cut magenta dress with a deep V-neck. A long cape was
casually thrown over her shoulders, and diamonds glittered
at her ears. Yet she and her friends, Nancy realized, looked
entirely out of place, as if they had dressed for a formal
evening in Athens rather than a provincial festival.

Longing to get away from them, she invited Niko to go
with her in search of Barbara and Panos. At the first *taverna* they entered, half a block from the shop, they found
them.

Nancy's spirits lifted as she joined them at their table. The
evening might be bearable after all, with her friends at her
side.

When she and Niko were seated, the owner hastened over
with newly bottled wine, as well as a plate of feta cheese and
black olives. In celebration of the grape harvest, the wine

was free that night all over town, and on this occasion it was considered appropriate to get a little tipsy, if not drunk. Even children were allowed their share in the festivities, so Niko was poured a small glass of wine of his very own.

Before long, Nancy found her tension dissolving and her bruised ego healing itself. The wine and the music got to her, and she became caught up in the bacchanalian spirit that pervaded. Barbara and Panos took her on the rounds of the *tavernas*, where they drank more wine and consumed the food set out for them by the owners or their wives.

At a relatively modern *taverna* beside the harbor, Nancy found herself greeted by several of the people she had come to know on her frequent trips to town. Dimitri, the waiter at the café in the square, addressed her by name. With him was his sister, Alexandra, the woman Nancy had chatted with at the post office, and at the same table were Petros and Giorgos, the shoemakers who had fixed Nancy's sandal strap. Nancy responded to their friendliness, using the increasingly numerous Greek phrases she was learning.

She and Niko, with Barbara and Panos, sat at a table by the door. By now she was fully relaxed and enjoying herself, the quarrel with Kostas out of her mind. Several men, slightly intoxicated, were dancing the *sirtaki*.

Niko turned to Nancy, his eyes shining. "I will be well enough to dance soon, will I not, Nancy?"

"You're strong enough now," she answered, taking his hand in hers. "You could dance, if you wanted."

"But I cannot. I would look foolish with a leg that does not bend."

"Does it matter how you look? It's your enjoyment that ought to count."

Panos leaned across the table toward them. He had to speak loudly in order to be heard over the music. "In that case, Nancy, why do you not both get up to dance?"

"But I thought it was traditional for men to dance alone," she said, secretly longing to get up and join the dancers.

"Except that you are a foreigner and not expected to ad-
here to our local customs. Besides, it gives us great pleasure
to see our guests enjoying themselves. The whole town will
take it as a compliment to their music and their wine."

"Very well, Panos," she said, eager to move to the com-
pelling rhythm. "You asked for it. But it will be your fault
if I look silly. Come on, Niko, we're going to dance."

Niko demurred at first, then with a pleased smile, rose
from his chair. At once there was a scattering of cries from
the surrounding tables.

"Bravo, Niko," she heard, and "Bravo, *Americanida*."
They were being cheered on by the townspeople, and under
a barrage of good-natured heckling, Nancy and Niko joined
the line of dancers.

Although she was sure they appeared slightly comical, no
one laughed at them—at least not as far as she could tell.
Niko limped through his movements, while Nancy had to
learn as she went along, watching the feet of the other
dancers. But appearances, for the moment, mattered to no
one, and by the time they were beginning a second dance,
they were both breathless and laughing, enjoying themselves immensely.

Suddenly there was a stir at the entrance. Even without
looking up, Nancy knew who had come in. She had been
unconsciously dreading their appearance ever since she had
gone off with Niko in search of Barbara and Panos. Loukia swept in first, trailing her magenta cloak, followed by
Katina and Martin and the others. When they were all in
and converging on the only empty table, she saw Kostas.

All the color seemed to drain out of the room as he
paused in the doorway, his brilliant dark eyes sweeping the
assemblage. He took in Barbara and Panos at their table
and acknowledged them with a nod of the head. Then his
eyes moved across the line of dancers, stopping to rest on
her and Niko.

He looked displeased as he drew near, and she wondered
what he intended to do. In the dangerous mood he'd been

in earlier, he might well yank them both from the floor and send them home as if they were children.

She was astounded when he met her eyes and smiled, his austere face relaxing into handsome lines. Then he stepped between her and Niko, unlinked their arms and joined the dance.

There was nothing for her to do but put her arm, which had been resting on Niko's thin shoulders, across the taller and broader shoulders of his brother. She could feel the hardness of his muscles through his silk shirt. And as she noticed this, she became dimly aware that Loukia was sitting at the nearby table with her hard eyes focused on them.

Then the music and the wine and the festivity of the evening took hold of her. Kostas's presence, the pressure of his hand on her shoulder, the heat from his body as he danced in the hot smoke-filled room, gave her boundless confidence. She felt capable of anything, now that he was beside her, able even to perform to perfection the intricate steps of the dance. The movements seemed to come naturally as she let the music sweep her away.

All memory of the bitter words they had exchanged earlier was erased, and she felt as she had the night at the temple. For there *was* an unspoken bond between them. It pulled at her senses so powerfully that she was certain the entire roomful of people must feel it, too. And in the face of that bond, none of her warnings to herself about him mattered. She had lost all sense of anything but the pleasure of the moment.

The music seemed to go on forever, and Nancy saw nothing but the floor in front of her, felt nothing but that strong yet gentle arm on hers. But at last the musicians stopped. The perspiring dancers returned to their tables, their friends and the freely flowing wine.

"There is nothing you do not do well," Kostas said as he led her and Niko back to their table.

Touched by his unexpected praise, she looked up into his face. It seemed as if they had become two different people from the man and woman who had argued so bitterly only a short time before. She didn't understand how or why the change had come about, but basking in the good feeling of the moment, she accepted it without question.

Kostas greeted Barbara and Panos in a friendly manner, then left to join Loukia at the table she had chosen at the other side of the room.

As Nancy helped the tired Niko into his chair, she heard a disturbance. Loukia's voice came across the room, her words quite clear even over the noisy drinkers.

"It's too hot in here, Kostas! Let's leave this stuffy place and go back home where we can breathe."

Nancy couldn't make out his reply, but Loukia was standing and gathering her cape around her. She swept out haughtily, the rest of the party standing to follow her with what seemed to Nancy to be reluctance.

"Isn't she a horror!" Barbara exclaimed. "Did you see the way everyone was looking at her getup?"

"No," Nancy admitted truthfully. She had been too filled with her own impressions and feelings to pay attention to Loukia.

"You look ten times better than she ever could," Barbara went on vehemently. "And don't think Kostas didn't notice."

"And why should he not?" Panos replied charmingly, as they, too, rose to leave. "Nancy is the second most beautiful woman on the island tonight—after you."

"A born diplomat!" Barbara laughed, moving to give him a kiss on the cheek. "You should be running the country, sweetheart, instead of a stationery shop."

The car was gone when Nancy and Niko reached the spot where it had been left. Apparently Loukia had insisted on returning home at once. Although Nancy was sure Kostas would return for them, Panos insisted on driving her and the boy. Exhausted, she leaned her head against the back of the seat and chatted comfortably with Barbara and Panos, until at last they found themselves in front of the Paradissis house.

"Are you as tired as I am, Niko?" she asked as they watched the car go back over the hill toward town.

He yawned. "I cannot wait to get into my bed. Wine makes me sleepy."

But the evening was not over for them yet, for the others were gathered in the salon, where Kostas had poured brandy for them. Niko looked very pale, with dark circles once again visible under his eyes. Nancy hoped he hadn't seriously overtired himself, but she thought it best he please his brother by joining the company for a few more minutes. Niko could catch up on sleep in the morning, she thought.

As they advanced into the room, Loukia, looking regal in a thronelike chair, gestured to Niko with long graceful fingers.

"Niko, come to Loukia." When he drew near, she put an arm around him, and in a whisper that everyone could hear, said seductively, "It is very hot indoors. Why don't you and I go swimming?"

Nancy, who was just reaching out for the brandy glass Kostas offered her, held her breath, wondering what Niko would say to this peculiar invitation. She watched him hesitate, looking from Kostas to her, weighing his exhaustion against Kostas's demand that he be polite to Loukia.

At last he nodded. "All right, Loukia. I will go with you." Only Nancy detected the quaver in his voice, his face full of reluctance.

Loukia's laugh chimed forth. "How lovely!" she exclaimed. "Niko and I have a rendezvous. Isn't that charming? Now, who else will join us in our midnight swim? But you must all swim with us, for it is a lovely night for swimming."

The others responded enthusiastically and rose to get their suits. In the flurry of activity, Nancy went over to the boy. She didn't like to interfere between him and his future sister-in-law, but her duty was to see to his well-being.

"Niko, don't you think you've had enough activity for one night? I know you want to please Loukia, but I'm sure she wouldn't expect you to go if you're too tired."

She must have spoken more loudly than she had thought, for Loukia stood up haughtily before the boy could reply, and with a great show of affection, threw an arm around his shoulders, hugging him to her. Nancy saw her necklace push against the skin of his cheek, but Niko obviously didn't dare to pull away, although the sharp metal was undoubtedly uncomfortable.

"Don't you think you're overstepping your authority?" Loukia asked condescendingly. "The boy doesn't want to go to bed so early when he's obviously perfectly well. A child his age must have a little fun on occasion."

"I'm sorry," Nancy said with conviction, quelling her nervousness at having to contradict Loukia, "but he's been fighting a cold, and it has been a long evening. It's dangerous for him to swim this late when he's so tired."

Loukia turned to the boy. "You do want to go with me, darling, don't you?" she asked again.

The boy paused a moment, once more looking from Loukia to Nancy, uncertain what to do. Then he nodded.

"There, you see?" cried the Greek woman triumphantly.

Nancy started to object, but suddenly Kostas cut in. "Leave him alone, Nancy!" he said in a cold voice. "Niko will swim."

Stung by his command, Nancy stood motionless, incapable of saying a word. The few who had returned to the room stopped talking, and Nancy felt their eyes on her.

"But Kostas—" she began, desperate to reason with him on a matter that concerned her professional judgment.

Again he cut her off before she could finish. "I said, leave him alone!"

There was no arguing with him. With tears stinging her eyes, Nancy turned and fled.

She hurried down the hall toward her room, glad to have escaped the eyes of all those people before the inner storm broke. She wouldn't want Kostas to know that he had made her cry.

Just as she put her hand on her doorknob, she sensed someone in the hall behind her. She whirled around just as Kostas reached her. He gripped her shoulders, his fingers pressed into her flesh. Furious that he had followed her, she tried to shake him off.

"What do you want?" she gasped.

"I have told you," he answered, his voice like steel, "that I will not have my brother coddled and made into an invalid!"

In her frustration, Nancy felt like striking him. "You are blind!" she cried, making a fist of her hand. "Couldn't you see he didn't want to swim? He's only trying to please you by pleasing Loukia. He's willing to do everything you ask, even if it means endangering his health."

"You make too much of his health." His mouth formed an angry grimace. "I tell you, Niko will be a man!"

"You unfeeling, insensitive brute," she cried, this time actually striking his chest with her fist. Pulling free of his grasp, Nancy backed up against the door. "You think swimming makes a man? You think courting danger makes a man? Niko is more of a man—a feeling sensitive man— than you could ever be!"

Her fit of temper suddenly gave way to tears, and she started to sob uncontrollably.

Kostas's eyes narrowed as he saw the hot tears flowing down her cheeks. Drawing in his breath sharply, he pulled her to him.

Nancy felt her senses reeling in his embrace. All she was aware of was his warm hard body pressed against hers, the beating of his heart against her breast.

"Unfeeling, am I?" he whispered, pulling away a little. Then he kissed her, his mouth moving insistently over hers, his lips forcing hers apart, his tongue exploring the soft recesses of her mouth. When he pulled away, they stood in the dim hallway simply staring at each other, their breath coming in jagged gasps.

Tearing herself away, Nancy turned to open the door. As she did so, she caught a glimpse of magenta at the salon door. Loukia stood there, watching.

Nancy threw herself on her bed, buried her face in her pillow and sobbed. What kind of man could treat a woman the way Kostas treated her—humiliating her and then plundering her senses with such a kiss? For his kiss was not one of love, but his way of showing he was the master and could do as he pleased. How she hated him!

She was at her lowest point. Although she told herself she ought to get up and stop giving in so foolishly to self-pity, she was unable to stop weeping. All she was capable of doing was lying on her bed with tears streaming down her cheeks until the spell passed. And at last it did pass. The sobbing subsided, and she lay quietly in the dark room, spent, her wet face pressed against the pillow.

Outside her window she could hear laughter and shouts from the swimmers. Selfish people, she thought, concerned only for their own pleasure, while they disturbed Kiki's sleep and endangered Niko's health. She knew that strenuous overexertion would set back the progress he had made. If only Antonis were back. She was certain he would have taken her part and seen to it that Niko did not swim that night. Unfortunately, the head of the family was not due back for a few more days. In the meantime, the merrymakers could do their damage, heedless of the consequences or the needs of the rest of the household.

More than an hour later she heard the revelers coming up the path, almost as noisily as ever. And at last, when the house was silent, she rose and switched on her light.

In the mirror, she could see that the yellow dress was crushed in front where she had lain on it, and her eyes were red and puffy from the weeping. Slowly, with the little energy she had left, she unzipped the dress and put it over the back of the chair. She pulled off her underclothes and went into her bathroom, where she washed her face, brushed her teeth and ran a comb through her hair. Then, longing for the oblivion of sleep, she climbed into bed and switched off the light.

But sleep did not come. She lay there staring up at the dark ceiling for what seemed like hours, until she couldn't lie still any longer. She rose and crossed to the window. Opening the shutter, she sat gazing out at the inky water and the cypress trees swaying in the night breeze.

She wondered what she would be feeling right now if *she* were Loukia, alone in her room after a day in which she had contrived to get her own way in everything, to satisfy every whim that crossed her mind. Did the Greek woman ever bother with self-recrimination, she wondered. Did she ever suffer quietly, as Nancy was doing, unwilling and unable to burden anyone else with her troubles? Probably she lay in bed thinking of her future life with Kostas, smug and satisfied that, as in all things, she was bound to get her own way in this marriage.

This marriage. Nancy's heart gave a painful lurch. What would it be like to be Kostas's fiancée? As fierce jealousy wracked her body, Nancy suddenly realized that more than anything in the world she longed to change places with Loukia. Kostas Paradissis was arrogant, temperamental and opinionated—and also the most exciting and complex man she had ever met. And in a moment of blinding clarity, she knew that she had fallen hopelessly in love with him.

Nancy sat at her window staring out into the dark silent night. How fickle happiness was. When she first realized she would be coming to Greece, her joy had been boundless. And Korpas itself, with its simple beauty, had filled her with elation. Waking up to the fresh morning air, feeling the sensual pleasure of running in the soft sand or swimming in the sea—that had been, for her, enough, and she had felt she could never ask for anything more.

Now her realization had changed everything. The island was still magnificent beyond words. The sand and sea lay below her window under a starry sky, unaltered. Yet they no longer had the power to fill her soul with joy. Happiness now, she thought sadly, would only be to see Kostas Paradissis's eyes shining with love for her.

How had it happened? She cupped her face in her hands, and her lovely hazel eyes clouded. Her newly acknowledged love amazed her so that she was unable to comprehend how it had begun. She had been prepared to dislike him from the start—even in New York when he had broken his promise to Niko. And then, to reinforce her negative feelings, his treatment of her had been anything but cordial. He had made his disapproval clear from the beginning. Yet, there was that strange bond between them.

Nancy's pulse quickened at the memory of the evening at the temple. Then she saw Kostas as he had looked underwater, so graceful despite his masculine strength. She had felt that unspoken bond then, too. From the moment she had first met him on the dock, Nancy's feelings had swung like a pendulum. One moment Kostas infuriated her and she was sure she should have nothing more to do with him. Then the next she found herself so powerfully drawn to him she was afraid of losing her senses completely. And now there was no escaping the fact that she loved him—and all the beauty that was Greece was not enough to comfort her.

Kostas would never be hers. Even if he weren't betrothed to Loukia, he had made it clear he would never consider marriage to a foreigner. She was a foreigner, and as such, he would never completely trust her. If only she could have been that first American woman he had loved. She would never have given him that dreadful ultimatum. She would never have wounded him.

She sighed and leaned her forehead against the window. When her work with Niko was done, she would return to New York. But Niko would stay here—and now she knew his fears for the future were grounded in reality. After the marriage, Loukia would become mistress of the house, and Nancy could well imagine what that would mean. She was not the sort to preserve its simple beauty, nor could she be counted on to care for Niko properly. Yet the difficult time for the boy would only last a few years, and then he would be free to embark on his own life. But for her the future would be constant pain. No matter where she was, Nancy knew she would continue to love Kostas and to ache for what could never be.

As she began to close the shutters, Nancy heard soft voices below her window. She looked out and saw two figures standing close together on the beach. Loukia's silvery laughter stabbed at Nancy's heart.

She felt a kind of despair she hadn't experienced since she was a child, when, returning home after a weekend at her aunt's house, she had been told there was an accident and she would never see her parents again. She had not thought of that day and its pain for years. Yet now it all came flooding back to her—how she had sat alone in her room all that day, unable to eat, unable to find the energy to do anything but sit by the window, watching as the sunny morning clouded up and then rain streaked the glass, obscuring the view. She had felt only numbness and absolute grief, beyond tears, beyond words, beyond any kind of action.

Did being in love with Kostas mean opening herself up to that mind-numbing kind of pain? How she wished she had never met him. How she longed to go back in time and erase forever the circumstances that had brought her there. She could never have Kostas—yet to be without him meant a future deprived of real happiness, of real meaning. She could never replace her parents, but had had to compensate for their absence as best she could. And considering her loss, her childhood had been smooth, thanks to Jan. Yet she had always been painfully aware of the void left by their deaths—an emptiness no amount of friends or sisterly love could fill. Was it now to be the same for her in adulthood? Would she be forever without the love she wanted?

She stared the cruel reality of a loveless future full in the face without letting herself flinch. There was no future for her with him, and continuing in his presence now that she knew she loved him could only mean more misery—far worse misery than facing her pain alone in New York. Her self-respect would not allow her to remain in the same house with him after what had happened. Besides, to have her professional judgment so brutally challenged made her job impossible. She was a trained physical therapist and a good one, and she took pride in her ability. She could not continue to work effectively where her efforts were undermined by others.

She would leave as soon as Niko was well, she decided. She knew that that time was imminent—might, in fact, already be here, if he had gone swimming in the dark tonight without mishap.

Meanwhile, she must get through the remaining days with as much of her self-respect as possible still intact. She must minimize her contact with Kostas and stop thinking about him when she was alone. In this way she might return to New York with dignity and as few regrets as possible. She could cry over her lost happiness later.

At long last she turned away from the window and the beauty of the night and climbed into her bed.

CHAPTER ELEVEN

IN THE MORNING, during exercises, she watched Niko closely. His legs had grown very strong, and when they walked down the path to the beach for their swim, his limp was almost imperceptible.

"How was your swimming last night?" she asked him as they waded into the sea. "Any difficulty?"

He turned toward her with a face that had suddenly grown very grave. He seemed more and more adult to her every day.

"No difficulty," he replied, "but it was no fun. I was very tired and only went to please Loukia. But tell me, Nancy...I do not understand why my brother spoke to you the way he did. Why would he be so...so hard with you? He is not like that normally. Does he not see what a good friend you are to this family? I am thinking I must speak to him about it."

"Niko, please don't," she shot back, alarmed. "It's between Kostas and me, and you mustn't get involved. Your brother has made up his mind about me, and nothing anyone can say will change it. He thinks I'm only interested in you because of the money your father pays me. He doesn't understand how dearly I love you and how much my sister needs that financial help."

"And I love you, Nancy."

She smiled. "The truth is, Niko, that you are almost well, and I'll have to leave soon."

"I do not want you to go. If I do not get well, you will have to stay, will you not?"

"We'll have to accept my leaving and be grown-up about it when the time comes," she replied.

Niko's trusting face regarded her seriously, and he appeared to be deep in thought. Then, he seemed to shake himself out of his preoccupation, and taking her hand, headed toward the water.

They swam about a mile together, much farther than she had ever gone with Niko, certain that he was now strong enough to take it. They raced out to the point below the temple, rested on the rocks and then swam leisurely back. She savored every moment of her time with him, knowing that her stay was drawing to a close.

Once she looked up at the house and could see that the shutters of the guest rooms were beginning to be opened. Loukia had come out in her elegant housecoat to sit on the veranda, undoubtedly waiting for Kiki to bring her breakfast, as the little servant would have to do for each of the guests as they saw fit to make an appearance.

Niko was swimming past her, racing toward the beach with a spurt of energy. Reaching the shore before her, he stood and began climbing the sloping rocky floor.

Suddenly his voice screamed in pain, a cry that echoed against the rocks and flat water and rang out over Nancy's head. Then he crumpled before her horrified eyes.

"Niko!" Nancy cried, her heart feeling as if it had stopped beating.

In an instant, adrenaline was pumping through her body as she lunged forward in the water to cover the last few yards in a powerful crawl. Trembling with fear, she struggled to her feet, rushing through knee-deep water toward the small figure that writhed in pain in the shallows.

"Niko, I'm coming," she cried. She was barely aware of the shouts coming from the house where Loukia was running back and forth along the veranda, pointing toward them and screaming for Kostas.

When she reached him, Niko was very pale. His face was twisted with pain as he reached for her hand.

"I stepped on something sharp," he gasped.

"Can you stand up?" Nancy asked.

From the corner of her eye, she saw Kostas running down the path toward them, with Loukia and several of the others behind him.

Niko took her hand and squeezed it hard. "I cannot get up, Nancy. It hurts so very much." His face was contorted in his effort not to cry.

Now Kostas had waded out to them, his slacks soaked to the knee. "Put your arms around my neck, Niko," he said in the gentlest tone Nancy had ever heard from him. "I am going to lift you."

The boy did as he was told, and with a swift movement that required a good deal of strength, Kostas scooped his brother up and carried him, dripping, onto the sand.

"You should have hired a lifeguard instead of a nurse, Kostas!" Loukia said excitedly as he put the boy down and began to examine his foot. "What would have happened to the poor child if you hadn't been home? *She* couldn't possibly have carried him out of the water!"

Kostas said nothing, but began probing the foot with his fingers while Niko winced in pain at each touch, biting his lip to keep from crying out.

"It was only a sea urchin," Kostas said, looking up into Nancy's face. She saw the tremendous relief in his eyes and knew that hers were registering the same emotion. "I will remove the spines and bandage the foot."

Loukia turned to Nancy, her face almost triumphant. "Didn't you know better than to let him walk on those rocks? There are hundreds of sea urchins there."

"It was an accident, Loukia. It could have happened to anyone," Nancy said, defending herself against this unexpected and unwarranted attack.

Her eyes flew to Kostas. She hoped he would corroborate her words and assure Loukia she had not been negligent in her duty. But Kostas seemed too wrapped up in Niko, helping the boy to his feet and walking with him up the path, the boy leaning against his older brother's arm.

Nancy lagged behind the others going toward the house, for she felt a terrible weight crushing her spirit. She could

not believe that when Loukia had accused her of negligence, not one of the other adults had come to her defense.
What kind of people were these, anyway, she wondered
helplessly.

As if to prove what kind of woman *she* was, Loukia began speaking about Nancy to the others, as though she were
not there.

"After all," she told Katina, who was standing on the
veranda in her negligee, "she's only hired help, like Kiki.
Her problem is, she gives herself airs, as if living with her
betters has brought her up to their level."

"But, Loukia," ventured Katina timidly from the breakfast table, "Nancy is trained in physical therapy. She has
made Niko well, I understand."

Loukia's look was withering. "It's still a trade, like shoe-
making. There are bad shoemakers, aren't there?"

With that, everyone giggled. Kostas, with the boy's arm
across his shoulder, stopped in the doorway. He turned to
look at the friends of his fiancée in their various stages of
attire. His eyes went from one to the other as they all fell silent, and when his eyes swept past Loukia to Nancy's, she
felt a surge of hope that he would defend her against the vi-
cious attack.

But he did not. His face looked determined and purpose-
ful when he spoke. "Katina," he ordered, "go to Kiki for a
sterile needle and some bandages. Loukia, come with me."
He went into the house with his arm tenderly wrapped
around the boy.

Nancy's heart sank. Did Kostas, too, believe her guilty of
negligence? Why else would he not speak up to Loukia?
And to push the point home, he was going to dispense with
her services as a nurse altogether. It was Loukia who was
going to help remove the spines from the boy's foot, rather
than her. Loukia, of all people!

Nancy remained on the veranda after the others had gone
in. Her hands and feet were cold, despite the hot sun. She
had thought last night that she had reached her lowest point,
but now she knew that was not true. Last night had only

been a prelude to today, and now it seemed suddenly clear that all she had done out of love for Niko was entirely unappreciated, that her skill was regarded as negligible by them all. The fact that Kostas shared their low opinion of her was too much to bear.

Somehow she got through the midday meal with the others, saying little and trying not to show her hurt feelings as they went on with their bright, careless chatter. When it seemed to her that everyone had gone to nap after the meal, she went out the double doors of her room and along the veranda to look in on Niko. He was, after all, still her patient—even if she was the only one who saw it that way.

She peered through the open door and saw Niko asleep on the bed, covered with a light blanket, his face pale. A lock of hair had fallen across his forehead. Even in sleep, the traces of pain were not entirely erased. There were little lines at the corners of his mouth and between his eyebrows. How frightening he must have looked after his diving accident, when he had been in pain almost continually. And how she loved him! Her heart went out to him and she stepped forward, toward his bed, so she could smooth that face, remove all traces of pain.

But as soon as she entered the room, she saw that Niko was not alone. Loukia was sitting in an armchair against the wall. When she saw Nancy, the other woman closed the magazine she had been reading and languidly set it down on the table next to her.

"I'm sorry," Nancy stammered, turning to go out. "I didn't know anyone was in here with Niko."

"Kostas asked me to sit with the poor boy," Loukia whispered in answer. She put a finger to her lips, then rose slowly. "We must not talk in here," she said, stepping toward the door. "We might wake the child. Come outside.

"Of course, we all appreciate your concern for Niko," Loukia continued as she stepped onto the veranda with Nancy and shut the door behind them. "But I shall have the task of looking after him from now on. Let me save Kostas the trouble of telling you that your services are no longer required here—if, indeed, they ever were."

Nancy was absolutely stunned. The charcoal eyes that could look so soft and yielding when they regarded Kostas were knife sharp now.

"Niko is still my responsibility, Loukia," Nancy countered stiffly. "Antonis Paradissis hired me, and he has not dismissed me yet."

"Oh, yes, we all know about *that*." A graceful hand went up in an affected gesture, as if to stifle the laugh that came out shrill with contempt. "I wonder if Antonis's sharp mind isn't softening with age. You must have been very persuasive to talk him into it—but I suppose your type is good at that."

"My type?" Nancy kept her voice down with difficulty, concerned lest Niko somehow wake up and overhear this confrontation. "What type is that?"

"It's perfectly clear," Loukia said lazily, stretching her bronzed arms above her head and yawning. "But your efforts to get Kostas won't work the way they did on the old man. Really, if you weren't so clumsy in your pathetic plays for Kostas, it would be most amusing."

"You mean you think I'm here because of Kostas? Because of their money?" she asked in disbelief.

"Come, you don't have to pretend with me. I can see what you're up to. I told you. I saw the way you threw yourself at him at the wine festival. If you only knew how absurd you looked at that *taverna* dancing with all those men like one of the tourist girls panting after the local gigolos."

She stopped to laugh, as though enjoying the memory. "Fortunately," she went on, "it won't work because Kostas can see through you. He may play with you, if you know what I mean—but he'd never take someone like you seriously."

"You're wrong, Loukia," Nancy finally answered indignantly, "Kostas knows how I feel about Niko."

"My dear, I'm his fiancée. Don't you think he's talked to me about you? I know exactly what he thinks, and if I were you, I'd pack up at once and leave this island. You were never needed here and most certainly not wanted. You'll only make yourself more ridiculous if you remain. I tell you this for your own good."

Tears of rage stung Nancy's eyes, but she swallowed her pride in order to make one point that was more important to her than straightening out any misconception on Loukia's part. "When I do leave, Loukia," she said, "I hope you will be kind to Niko. He needs love very, very much. Be the friend he needs."

Then she stumbled off, blinded by her tears as she walked the length of the veranda to her own door. But before she went in, she heard the scraping of a chair on Kostas's balcony above her.

Once in her room, her mind began racing, making a plan of action. There was no point in staying a day longer—Loukia was right about that. By stationing Loukia in the room to see to it that her new status was clear, Kostas had shown that he, too, believed the accident was due to her carelessness.

She would take the morning ferry. Perhaps she could explain to Niko's father by letter, or somehow find his office in Athens and see him there. Surely, Antonis Paradissis wouldn't expect her to remain under these circumstances, her work haunted by suspicion.

She pulled her suitcase out of the closet but could not bring herself to begin the task of packing. Leaving the suitcase open on the bed, she moved to the chair by the window and sat. Looking out at the sea, she was filled with an empty grief at the knowledge that this would be her last day in Korpas.

BY MORNING, when the sun came up over the horizon and flooded the sea and beach with its brilliance, the little room looked as bare and impersonal as it had the day she arrived. All her belongings were packed in the two large brown suitcases. Gone were the toiletries and photographs of her family that had adorned the dresser and the mementos she had picked up in town. Each item she had packed brought back memories of precious times, and she had had to fight to keep the tears back. It would be another flawless day on Korpas, only she would not be there to enjoy it. She would have to be content with memories, for in less than two days she would be back in New York.

She sighed at the thought of resuming life in the city. The stay in Greece, which had started out so gloriously, was ending dismally. It would have been better, she thought bitterly, had she never come at all.

Loukia and her friends normally rose late, so there was no one at the breakfast table when Nancy sat down. Niko, Kiki told her, was still asleep in his room. The little servant set a basket of warm rolls on the table along with the ceramic coffeepot. Nancy watched her with affection. How she would miss her, that cheerful, bustling little person whom she thought of as a friend.

"You would like some cheese, Nancy?"

"No, thank you, Kiki," Nancy replied. She had no appetite, not even for the crusty rolls and homemade marmalade she loved.

Absently, she broke a piece of the roll and spread it with butter, so lost in thought that she did not hear the step of Antonis Paradissis until he was next to her.

"Good morning, Nancy. You are up early. Have you had your run already?"

"Mr. Paradissis!" she exclaimed. "I didn't know you had returned."

"I arrived yesterday evening," he said, taking the seat opposite her, "but some business kept me in town until quite late."

In the early morning light, his face showed a degree of strain and sleeplessness. Nancy anxiously searched for signs of disapproval, wondering if he knew about Niko's accident, and if he, too, held her responsible, as Kostas and

Loukia did. But the older man smiled warmly at her and took the cup of thick dark Turkish coffee Kiki handed him.

"Have you seen Niko yet?" she asked apprehensively.

"Yes. Kostas told me what happened when I came home. This morning when I looked in on him, he was sleeping peacefully. He is a strong boy. He will be well." As always, there was an unmistakable note of pride in his voice when he spoke of his sons.

"Mr. Paradissis," Nancy began tentatively, gathering her courage for the unpleasant task before her. "I'm happy you came back—I wanted very much to say goodbye to you in person."

"Goodbye?" The silver brows knit together in a perplexed expression.

"It would be best for me to leave because of what happened to Niko yesterday—"

"Please." He threw up a hand, interrupting her. "Do not think I hold you responsible for Niko's accident. I am very pleased with the progress Niko has made. He has improved faster than I had hoped, and I know it is due to your excellent care."

"Thank you," Nancy said, grateful for the sincere praise and tremendously relieved to find he did not blame her. "But Niko is coming along awfully well, and he really doesn't need me. It's time I got back to my own family in Connecticut."

The older man was watching her with his shrewd eyes. "You know that Niko will be upset by such a hasty departure. And frankly, I enjoy your lively presence in our home as much as he does. Why not stay longer? You are more than welcome to remain here as long as you like."

Looking into those wise eyes, Nancy knew she could not be dishonest with him. If nothing else, his kindness and confidence in her required that she be open.

"I can't stay," she said, choosing her words carefully. "Not even for Niko or you. My professional competency has been questioned. My presence is unwanted."

"Who has made you feel like this?"

She dropped her eyes. "Your son. Kostas." There was a silence, during which Nancy heard the soft hiss of the waves breaking on the shore.

"I see," he said at last.

She looked up to see Antonis Paradissis staring straight ahead, his fingers absently stroking his chin. "Kostas. Of course."

Then, as if musing aloud, he continued, "My sons are so different. Niko is like the sun. Bright, visible, bringing warmth. Kostas is the moon. Changeable, elusive and mysterious. Not ever easy to understand. And very easy to misinterpret."

"I think it was he who misinterpreted me," she burst out. "He seems to think I took this job only for the money."

"There was a woman once," he replied, "who unfortunately saw in my son a fortune rather than a man." Antonis's face saddened, and the lines seemed to deepen. Nancy saw how deeply he had felt Kostas's pain.

"But what does he have to fear from me?" Nancy asked incredulously. "After all, he's engaged to Loukia!"

"You must understand that although he seems modern Kostas is very traditional, as I myself am. In America, I know, it is thought old-fashioned to arrange matches. Romantic love is the basis for marriage there. But your country, you must admit, has a shockingly high divorce rate. This is what Kostas wishes to avoid, for the family is still sacred in Greece. Can you understand that?"

Nancy lowered her eyes, afraid he would see the sudden tears she felt welling. *How can I understand,* she thought sadly, *when it means that Kostas will marry Loukia, and I must return to the States?* The very thought filled her with anguish, for she knew she could never stop loving Kostas.

"Don't you believe in love?" she asked.

He reached across the table and patted her hand in a fatherly gesture. "I believe that true love is as beautiful as it is rare. Like a precious gem or a great work of art or nature. I myself was one of the lucky ones to know it does exist. Although my wife died many years ago, I wish with all my heart for my sons to know the same happiness I have known.

"However," he went on, "there are other important elements in marriage, such as common background and shared interests. Kostas wishes to marry a woman who shares his background, whose family is not unlike our own. At least, that is what he thinks he wants. I am not sure he is being wise."

He brought his eyes back to hers. "I am an old man," he continued, "but I am not blind. My old eyes see more, perhaps, than my son's young ones. I know that great mistakes can be made sometimes in the very process of trying to avoid them. But because my son is a man, he must live his own life, free of interference from his father. He must make his own mistakes."

Once again he took her hand, and in his face she saw a frank fatherly affection. "I will be sorry to see you go, Nancy. You have given Niko the love he never had from his mother, who died shortly after his birth. You have made a family out of the three of us. Will you not consider remaining here?"

Fighting back tears, she pushed back her chair and stood. "I've already packed my suitcases," she said. "I must take the morning ferry."

Antonis rose and embraced her in the Greek fashion, giving her an affectionate kiss on both cheeks.

"You will be missed," he said, "by all of us. May you find happiness."

As DIFFICULT AS SAYING GOODBYE to Antonis had been, the farewell to Niko was bound to be even harder. Nancy knew, as she headed down the hallway toward his room, that even if she were to be entirely truthful, there was no way he would understand her decision. And truthful she could not be, for she could not reveal her feelings about Kostas to him. Nor could she let him know how large a part Kostas had played in her decision to leave. Yet in any case she would have had to leave, she reminded herself, for Niko really was well on the road to recovery. Because she was no longer indispensable to him, she could leave with a clear conscience.

With these thoughts to give her courage, she knocked on the boy's door.

At his sleepy *"Peraste!"* she entered the room. The shutters were still shut, and he was lying in bed. How sweet he looked, she thought with a sudden motherly pang. His curly dark hair was tousled on the pillow, and she knew he looked much the way Kostas had as a young boy.

"Hi, Nancy," he said, propping himself up on one elbow.

She forced a smile and opened the shutters. Bright sunlight poured in, causing the boy to squint against the glare.

"How is your foot today?" she asked, sitting on the edge of his bed.

"It is much, much better," he said. "Only a little bit sore. Kostas fixed it very well, eh? He is better than a doctor!"

"Yes, it seems so," she replied.

"But maybe today I will rest," he went on, "and not do exercises. You would not mind, Nancy?"

"I think that's a good idea, Niko," she answered. "In fact, you are doing so well that before long you will not need to do any exercises at all."

Niko's face lit in one of his widest smiles. "That will make me happy, Nancy. Then I will be just as I was before."

"Yes, dear. And that's why I think that you really don't need me any longer. And so I'm going back home."

Niko's smile faded. He stared at her, uncomprehending, until his luminous eyes darkened and he reached for her hand. "You are going home? You are going away?"

"Yes, Niko. You know I promised Dr. Davies I would return to my job as soon as you were well."

His cry of anguish stopped her. "Why, Nancy? You said you would not leave if I was not well, and now I am injured again."

A new thought struck Nancy. "Did you step on that sea urchin on purpose, Niko?" she asked.

He gave her a sheepish look and ducked his face away from her. "I wanted you to stay," he said.

"Oh, darling," Nancy cried, near to tears herself as she heard his confession and understood to what lengths his desperation had driven him. "I know how much you want me to stay. But we will always go on being friends. We will write to each other often, and who knows, maybe when your father takes a business trip to New York, you'll come with him."

"No!" the boy exclaimed. "Everyone I love leaves. I thought you were different, that you would stay with me forever!"

She could think of nothing to say in the face of his emotion, and so she held him like a small child, gently stroking his soft hair.

"You know," she said at last, "it's difficult for me, too, Niko. This is the most difficult goodbye I've ever had to say. But leaving those we love is always painful. Sometimes I think all life is a series of goodbyes. Our loved ones die, like my parents and your mother, or the people we become close to must leave us for one reason or another. It's a part of life, and we must accept it and go on. You know I'll never forget you, Niko. And you know my time here with you will always be in my heart."

Niko pulled away and faced her. "I will tell Kostas," he threatened. "Kostas will make you stay."

"No, Niko!" Nancy said firmly. "Don't do that."

"Why not?" Niko's innocent face had taken on a shrewd and appraising expression, like his father's. "Why are you afraid of Kostas?"

"I'm not afraid of him, Niko. But I'm certain Kostas won't be sorry to see me leave."

"Kostas will listen to me," Niko insisted stubbornly.

"Niko," Nancy explained, taking his hands in hers, "please don't do or say anything. Just accept that this is the way things must be."

"All right," he said softly, once again ducking his head away from her. "I will do as you say."

FROM THE TAXI, Nancy saw the staunch little figure of Kiki staring after her, her hand reaching up to wipe her eyes.

"It is not right," she had insisted as she carried her bags to the waiting car. "You are not doing the right thing. Kiki knows."

But it was too late. Nancy had made her goodbyes as best she could. Now there was the town to face, the buying of boat tickets, her farewell to Barbara.

"Just like that?" Barbara demanded. "You're leaving just like that?" She stood in the middle of the narrow aisle of the shop, her face incredulous, her hands on her hips.

"I have to," Nancy repeated for the third time. "Don't you see?"

"No," her friend said adamantly. "I see that you've been subjected to a lot of abuse from that horrid woman. I see that you've been misjudged. But I do not see that you have to leave."

"Barbara, please," Nancy begged. "Don't make it any harder."

Barbara came over to her and put her arms around Nancy, much as Jan would have. "You love him, don't you?" she said softly. "That's the real reason you're going."

Nancy nodded miserably. "It's hopeless," she sighed. "Even if he loved me in return, he couldn't marry me. The only thing I can do is leave. Remaining here would be unbearable."

"God, how miserable," Barbara commiserated, putting her cheek against Nancy's. "And how I am going to miss you!"

All of a sudden there was an ear-splitting blast from the harbor, signaling the approach of the ferry. There was no more time for goodbyes, for the ferry had come somewhat earlier than expected. She'd have to make a dash for it, buying her ticket on board later.

Barbara helped her carry her suitcases to the dock, where a porter took over the task of putting them on board. Then Nancy and her friend embraced tearfully once more.

As Nancy made her way up the gangplank amid the crowds of people going to and from the mainland, she remembered the afternoon she and Niko had arrived. They had walked down that same gangplank, and she had seen Kostas for the first time, standing on the dock. He had seemed to her to be different from everyone around him, even then. No one else could have made her so miserable, for she loved him as she had never loved any other person. Would she ever be free of the pain of losing him, she wondered, or would everything from now on remind her of Kostas and bring this sharp stabbing ache to her heart?

Once on board, she bought her ticket from the purser and left the deck at once, eager to bury herself far from the sight of the island. She couldn't bear to watch it as it receded forever from her life. Finding a corner in the second-class lounge facing the white bulkhead, she sank down on a plastic seat and closed her eyes. A great sorrow took hold of her. The strain of the last twenty-four hours had exhausted her. First, there was Niko's accident and the horrible fear she had felt seeing him in so much pain. Then there were the difficult goodbyes to the people she had come to love.

Yet there had been no farewell to Kostas, not even a glimpse of him. Her last memory of him would be the tender way in which he carried Niko up from the sea.

Too upset to open her eyes, she dimly listened to the babble of voices around her, the ponderous and dignified Greek language she was now beginning to understand, mixed with the noises of the busy harbor.

Then there was another blast of the siren and the engines started up. She heard the clanking of the anchor and then felt the ship moving away from the dock.

She sighed. It was done and there was no turning back. The ferry was already on its way back toward the mainland she had left only weeks before. It was carrying her back to her old life, a life that seemed utterly desolate to her now.

All at once she felt a strange prickling sensation, as though she were not alone. Opening her eyes, she looked up to see Kostas standing over her.

His eyes blazed at her, and she shrank from their intensity.

"Kostas..." she began, confused by his unexpected appearance.

"What kind of woman are you!" he demanded.

"What do you mean?" she asked, struggling to gather her thoughts together. "Why can't you leave me alone? Haven't you hurt me enough already?"

He sat down next to her and forced her around to face him. Nancy saw anger in his eyes, a pulse throbbing at the hollow of his throat.

"What kind of woman," he demanded, "pretends to be so concerned with her duty, with the welfare of a young boy, only to abandon him?"

So that was it, she thought, her heart thudding. He still held her responsible for Niko's injury and regarded her leaving as cowardly. He had always looked for fault in her and would always find it where it did not exist.

She turned away, hurt and angry, biting her lip to keep from crying. There was nothing she could say. Nothing in the world would make him think better of her.

"Niko will be well soon," she answered in a flat empty voice, stripped of all desire to defend herself against him. She held no hope of ever getting through to him. "It's time for me to go home."

"To your sister in Connecticut, who has a family of her own? What kind of life will it be for you there?"

"What kind of life can it be for me here?" she demanded bitterly, swinging around to face him again. "Only a crazy person would stay where she isn't wanted, where she's accused of harming the very person she cares for the most."

He was quiet for a moment, and his eyelids came partway down, concealing the expression in his eyes.

"What are you saying?" he asked her. "Do you suppose for one minute that I blame you for what happened to Niko? I could see your face as you tried to get to him. I knew then how terrified you were that he might be seriously hurt. All the love you claimed to feel for him was there for me to read in your eyes. If I had any doubts about your affection for him, they were quelled at that moment."

"Then you really don't hold me responsible? But I thought—"

"You are too quick to jump to conclusions. You will have to learn to be more patient if you are to live on Korpas. This morning Niko told me how he 'happened' to step on the sea urchin. I was proud of him for doing what he did. He fought for what he wanted like a man, instead of giving in to what seemed inevitable."

"What do you mean, if I'm to live on Korpas?" she asked, not having heard a word after that.

The soft rich sound of his laughter flowed over her like warm water. "Do you suppose I mean to let you go? To lose my one chance for happiness?"

"But, Kostas . . ."

He took both her hands in his, and his black eyes softened. His expression, so tender after so much bad feeling between them, caused her to tremble.

"You were right about many things," he went on. "I was blind—blind to what mattered most to me in all the world. Even my little brother knew more than me. And Nancy—" he laughed suddenly at the memory "—what names he called me this morning after you left! Of course, I had already made up my mind."

"Made up your mind?" Her own mind was whirling, she couldn't keep pace with what he was saying, his new tone, the look in his eyes. Was this another swing of moods, to be followed by swift rejection?

"Why, made up my mind about you! That you were not as I thought—as I wanted to believe you were. Now I can tell you, Nancy Spaulding, how I want you. From the first moment I saw you, yelling in English at Yannis, the postman, to let Niko down the gangplank, I wanted you. And then later, in the moonlight, your alive eager eyes, your charm. But desire—even desire as strong as mine for you—is not enough. And I was engaged, with Loukia expected at any moment."

"Loukia!" She had forgotten all about the woman, lulled as she was by the unbelievable words she was hearing. "Kostas, you are still engaged."

"Was, Nancy. I overheard Loukia's conversation with you yesterday. I couldn't sleep—you and Niko were both weighing on my mind very heavily. I saw then what I was beginning to suspect—that Loukia has two faces, one for me and another for those she believes are beneath her. And there was another thing I realized at the same time. Loukia is very shrewd, very clever. She must have known what I didn't yet know—that I was in love with you and not with her. She was desperately jealous, and she did what she thought she had to do."

"Kostas." Nancy closed her eyes, then opened them again. "Kostas, is it true what you're telling me? That you're in love with me?"

He raised a hand and stroked the side of her face gently, as though she were a child. "How could you doubt it? You must have seen how I felt about you all along."

"You had a funny way of showing it. But maybe I did know, somewhere inside. Otherwise, how could I have fallen so very much in love with you?"

"I am so glad," he whispered into her ear, "for if I had to lose you, my life would never be complete. You are the most wonderful woman I've ever met."

She smiled up at him. "But I'm not Greek," she teased.

"Ah, my love, life is not always as we wish it. That is a drawback I will have to learn to live with."

His face held a radiance of love and a burning passion. Nancy, forgetting there was anything else on earth in that moment but the two of them, sat up and put a hand on his throat where the pulse beat rapidly. Then she touched his face, his thick curly hair.

His eyes on hers, he brought his face close to hers until she could feel his warm breath on her eyes, her mouth. Then his lips were on hers, heavy with desire, and she was kissing him back with all the ardor she had so long held back.

There was no telling what would have happened if they had been in some private room, alone together. But they were in the second-class lounge of the *Ikaros*....

"Kostas!" she cried suddenly, pulling away from his embrace. "Do something. We must be halfway to Athens."

He laughed, throwing his head back, his hand caressing the back of her neck. This was how she had wanted to see him—happy, relaxed, all his conflicts and moodiness gone. This was worth waiting for, worth suffering for.

"What can I do, my love? I cannot walk on water. We will just have to take a good long look at the Aegean before we go home. Do you remember what you said the first day you came to Korpas? You were on the veranda and you said to Kiki that she had the Aegean for her backyard."

Nancy laughed at the memory. "Yes. And you were out on your balcony and heard me."

Kostas pulled her to him once more. "And now, my love, do you think you would like the Aegean to be your backyard as well?"

Speechless with happiness, her heart flooded with love, she could only nod, her eyes bright with the future he was offering.

"Then you shall have it," he declared solemnly, his own eyes growing misty. "You shall have it for the rest of your life."

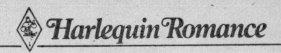 **Harlequin Romance**

Coming Next Month

2761 STRANGER IN TOWN Kerry Allyne
An Australian storekeeper is convinced all gold prospectors are daydreamers, living in a fantasy. Then, falling in love with one of them brings a change of mind—and heart!

2762 THE DRIFTWOOD DRAGON Ann Charlton
Haunted by his past, an Australian film star is overjoyed when he finds a woman whose love helps him to shed his typecast image—until his brother's interference almost ruins their chance for happiness.

2763 VOWS OF THE HEART Susan Fox
Returning for physical and emotional recovery to the Wyoming ranch where she'd always felt secure, an interior designer discovers her adolescent crush for its owner has turned to love.

2764 AMARYLLIS DREAMING Samantha Harvey
Katy finds a man on Amaryllis Island, but not the father she seeks. She finally has to admit, though, that this powerful island overlord is destined to make all her dreams come true.

2765 ASK ME NO QUESTIONS Valerie Parv
Trusting her adventurer husband once lead to heartbreak for a Brisbane art-gallery owner. Her return, years later, when she's thinking of marrying someone else, faces her with a once-in-a-lifetime choice.

2766 TO BRING YOU JOY Essie Summers
A living legacy gives a young New Zealander the chance to prove her descent from the historic Beauchamps. But her benefactor, dear Aunt Amabel, wants her niece to find adventure—and love.

Available in May wherever paperback books are sold, or through Harlequin Reader Service.

In the U.S.
P.O. Box 1397
Buffalo, N.Y.
14240-1397

In Canada
P.O. Box 2800, Postal Sation A
5170 Yonge Street
Willowdale, Ontario M2N 6J3